"Something smells good."

His voice was just behind her left ear, whispered instead of spoken. Hope turned around quickly.

"It's only bread," she protested, warding him off with both hands.

"That isn't what I was talking about," Ralph said as he put a hand on each of her shoulders and pulled her soft body up against his. "This is what I mean."

"Whatcha doin', Uncle Ralph?" Melody was standing in the doorway. "Marrying Miz Hope?"

He broke away and took a deep breath. "Marrying? Who ever thought of such a thing. I'm kissing the cook," he answered. "Just checking to see if she's done yet, you know. Like we have to test the bread."

"Is she done?"

"Oh, lord, the bread," Hope squeaked. The smell of fresh bread enveloped the kitchen, and just the tiniest bit of smoke. "The bread's done," she announced. *And so am I*, she teased herself. *So am I!*

Dear Reader,

Welcome to the latest book in our **Holding Out for a Hero** series. Every month for a whole year we'll be bringing you some of the world's most eligible men. They're handsome, they're charming but, best of all, they're single! And as twelve lucky women are about to discover, it's not finding Mr. Right that's the problem—it's holding on to him!

Hold out for a special Christmas hero in December:

Unexpected Engagement
by
Jessica Steele

Happy reading!

The Editors
Harlequin Romance

Some men are worth waiting for!

Bringing Up Babies

Emma Goldrick

Harlequin Books

TORONTO • NEW YORK • LONDON
AMSTERDAM • PARIS • SYDNEY • HAMBURG
STOCKHOLM • ATHENS • TOKYO • MILAN
MADRID • WARSAW • BUDAPEST • AUCKLAND

ISBN 0-373-03431-8

BRINGING UP BABIES

First North American Publication 1996.

Printed in U.S.A.

CHAPTER ONE

"AND so this is the end of Alfred?" Mary Kate Latimore looked up from her petit point as her youngest daughter paced in front of her, swinging her arms back and forth and occasionally pounding one fist into the other.

"Definitely," Hope said angrily. "The very end. But you won't tell Dad?"

Mary Kate laid her work aside and folded her hands. "Your father is a friend of Alfred's father," she said judiciously. "But that has nothing to do with whom or when or why you might date or marry, you know."

"But he said—"

"He? Alfred?"

"Yes. He said that my father wouldn't like it if I gave him the shove, and there'd be—well, he said there'd be hell to pay after he told Dad, and then he gave me that sneer of his and walked off, and—"

"Dear Lord, child! You've been sitting up all night worrying about such a thing? Surely you know your father better than that!"

"Sometimes I'm not sure, Ma. Everybody else in the family is big and tall and firm—" she swallowed to clear her throat and dash a tear away "—and the men they've married are the same. But me, I'm a shrimp if there ever was one—five foot nothing—"

"Almost like me," her mother interrupted. "And nice golden hair, the way mine used to be before it turned all gray. And a nice figure, to boot. What do you mean by *firm*?"

"Well, you all have—strong opinions, so to speak. But you know me, Ma, I've never had the guts to—I'm not like Becky. She's a doctor; I faint at the sight of blood. And I'm not like Mattie; she went to Africa, but I don't have the nerve even to go to Boston by myself. Or Faith; she's a lawyer—and married to a Texan construction man. I couldn't argue beans in a courtroom, and cows scare me half to death. I'm—I just don't have it in me to be anything. I couldn't hold down a school-teaching job although I love children. I couldn't even be a librarian. What's to become of me? Alfred?"

"You're young, child. You'll find a place," Mary Kate said. "You'll see. And it needn't be Alfred Pleasanton, either."

"Yeah," Hope said glumly. "In a convent, maybe?"

"Hush now, child." Her mother smiled at her. "With a temper like yours there's no room for you in any convent I know of." And then she said more firmly, "Sit down over here. Your dad just drove up."

"I'm going to hide somewhere," Hope said, jumping to her feet.

"Sit down." It was that voice of command that all the Latimore family knew. Hope snatched out a handkerchief and dropped into the lounge chair across from her mother, doing her best to look brave, and failing.

The big man who came through the door whistling was not what he once had been. His hair was totally gray, he seemed slightly bent at the shoulder, and he only went to Boston once a week, or whenever his son Michael called for help in running Latimore Incorporated, the biggest construction company on the East Coast.

Bruce Latimore came over to where his tiny wife was busy, leaned over, and kissed the top of her head. "Oh, what a day," he complained. "This arthritis business isn't all it's cracked up to be."

Mary Kate looked up and gave him an intimate smile. "It's not all that calm around here, either. If you'd taken your pills at lunchtime—"

He held up both hands over his head in a surrender signal. "I told you so?"

"I told you so," Mary Kate repeated. "*Your* daughter has a problem."

"*My* daughter?" Bruce Latimore knew one thing for sure. Mary Kate Latimore—Superior Court Justice Latimore—gave all the orders to the female side of his family, and only called on him when she needed him to repeat what she had already decided. Now all he had to do was figure out what she wanted him to say.

"Hope? You have a problem?"

The girl sat up straight in her chair, a difficult business, since all the chairs had been bought to fit her father's long legs. Her mother used a rolling footstool. Hope had become accustomed to balancing on the very front edge of the chair.

"Not exactly," she said softly. "I—" And then at high speed she confessed, "I broke off my engagement with Alfred."

"Ah." Bruce's brain went into high speed. "Alfred? He's that obnoxious twit who's been hanging around the house the past two months?"

"The very one," Mary Kate coached from the sidelines.

"Dad, I—"

"What a good idea," her father interrupted. "Couldn't stand his father either now that I think of it. That will give you more free time?"

Hope Latimore stumbled over her tongue. *More free time?* Her father had grown older, but not mentally slower. A girl who spoke without thinking in this family could be in a lot of trouble. But just that—more free time? How could that be a problem? She circled around the question a time or two, the way Rex, the family dog, circled his rug, and could find no obvious traps.

"Why—yes," she answered, staring down anxiously at the floor.

"Good," her father said. "I need some help."

Hope's eyes flashed up. Her father had dropped into his favorite chair and picked up the *Boston Globe*. Her mother's always busy hands had come to a stop as she looked across the room at her daughter. And then Mary Kate shrugged and went back to her petit point.

"You need some help?" It seemed almost impossible. For all her life she had watched her father run the world. Only occasionally had he turned to Mary Kate for advice. Even though her sister Becky had laughed at her, telling her that their mother *really* ruled the world, Hope had clung to her belief that Father was the one in charge. And now—

Her father put his newspaper aside. "Yes, I do, m'dear. You like children, don't you? Little ones?"

Hope crossed her fingers. "Yes," she said hesitantly. "*Little* ones, that is."

"So that's settled," Bruce Latimore said as he returned to his paper.

"What—what's settled?" Hope asked.

He put down his paper again. "Didn't I say?"

"No, I'm afraid you didn't, dear." Her mother's soft contralto voice was loaded with expression. Hope's head snapped around. Years of experience had taught her that Mary Kate Latimore was laughing at her—or her father—or both of them. Not a malicious or cutting laugh. Something more along the lines of a sympathetic laugh. But laughing all the same. "Perhaps you ought to explain yourself, Bruce."

"Yes, well..." He fumbled in his pocket for his pipe, knocked the bowl against his hand, and tucked the stem into the corner of his mouth. No tobacco. His wife had, when all the children were young, convinced him that smoking was bad for children. "I have this fellow—"

"A big, tall employee?"

Bruce looked startled. "Well, no, on both counts. He's a subcontractor, not an employee. And, everything considered, no, he's not very tall. About five foot eight or nine, I would guess."

Hope gave an audible sigh of relief, but refused to give up. "Not an employee?"

Her father grinned at her. "Something wrong with employees?"

"They have this tendency," Hope said solemnly. "Everything that goes in their ears comes out their mouths up in Latimore headquarters."

"Ah. Alfred?"

"That's *one* of his problems."

"As well as being too tall?"

Hope brushed aside her swathe of long blonde hair. "As well as," she admitted.

"Then this fellow is just what you need," her father said, chuckling. "He's just what the construction business has come to need too, but can't hire. A computer genius. There aren't many of them around. So we contract with him by the problem. And he doesn't come cheap."

"I'm sure you could find a woman to do the job as well," Hope snapped. "Does it always have to be a man?"

"No, it doesn't, but we've had experience with this young man—and your brother Michael trusts his judgment."

"Well..." Hope clasped her hands in her lap. "So why—?"

"He has a peculiar problem. His sister has two small children. A boy and a girl. And the sister and her husband were injured in an auto accident. Now that they're recovering, they need to give themselves time to recuperate fully—a leisurely holiday. And they don't have any family to look after the kids."

"And?"

"We need his expertise right now. He says he can't work because he's house-keeping. He says, in fact, that the only way he can execute our contract is if we provide a true and trustworthy—"

"Babysitter?" Hope interrupted.

"Housekeeper," her father qualified. "A couple—maybe three months. Two kids, both very young. Practically babies, I expect. They live down the highway about a mile north of Taunton."

"I could perhaps bring them up here?"

"He says no. The children have been living in his house since the accident. He doesn't want them to lose that comfort while their father and mother are away. The mother has been hospitalized for six months or more. He's worried that the little girl might not even remember her. Well, what do you think?"

What do I think? Hope ran the idea back through her brain as if she were playing a video tape. A settled family. Two little children. One adult male who would probably be working in Boston, of course. She could take Rex with her, just in case, and drive—

"Of course he expects you to live in," her father said, disrupting her chain of thought.

"You know, you don't *have* to work," Mary Kate said softly. "Your share of the dividends from Latimore Incorporated would—"

"Float a battleship. But I'd go mad without *something* to do," Hope said desperately.

"It starts tomorrow," her father said as he turned back to his paper.

"Just whoa now. Starts the day *after* tomorrow," Mary Kate said firmly. "This is my baby we're talking about. Tomorrow is the second of January. It's also the day that I go down to check out this young man."

Hope felt the need to fight back. "Michael is two years younger than me. *He's* the baby of the family," she said brashly.

Her mother put her work down and stared at her daughter. "Michael is three inches taller than your father, and has been running Latimore Incorporated for the past two years. *You* are my baby."

And for that Hope had only one answer. "Yes, ma'am," she said.

Sunday came, ushered in by a brilliant but cool sun, a chilling wind out of Canada, and a hint of more winter to come. The storm-battered trees, all long since stripped of their leaves, lined Route 138 southward, and Hope Latimore whistled to sustain her courage as she drove her black Jeep Wagoneer slowly toward Taunton.

Rex, her massively overweight German shepherd, sat in the seat adjacent to her, his nose sticking out into the breeze. Mary Kate had come back the day before with a frown on her face, but an approval on her tongue— "just so long as Rex is included in the party". It hardly made a great deal of sense, to Hope's way of thinking. Rex was fourteen years old, and could barely fight his way out of a brown paper bag; but just having this old friend along added a soupçon of courage to Hope's very limited bag of strengths.

About fifteen minutes down the road she spotted the house. Set far back from the road, almost out of sight from the highway, it was a comfortable-looking old farmhouse, with a multitude of additions that sprawled out in all directions. Hope maneuvered carefully off the paved road and up the dirt track that led to the front porch. The place was quiet, almost abandoned. And Rex refused to leave the vehicle.

"Coward," Hope muttered, and took a deep breath and went up the stairs. Her dog whined at her, but stirred not a muscle. The old oak door had a ringer-type doorbell. The kind you twist and it rings as it runs down. No batteries required. So she gave it a twist, and then another.

There was a little explosion from behind the door. A swelling of chatter as the door swung open. And two little people. Well, perhaps not all that little. A husky boy and a dainty little girl. The boy was almost a head shorter than Hope, the girl more than a head shorter than the boy.

"Well?" the boy inquired with a snarl.

"I—" Hope swallowed hard. Her throat was dry. She had never been good at initial meetings. "I'm the new— housekeeper," she said.

"Hah!"

Which was exactly Hope's feeling. She took a step backward, and almost fell down the stairs. The two children stared at her with wide dark eyes.

"My very own father lied to me," Hope muttered. "He said you were babies!"

"Hah!" The boy stepped out on the porch and looked her up and down. "Babies? I'm eight and Melody is three. Babies?"

"No, I can see—" Hope started to explain, just as Rex vaulted out of the car and walked up to stand behind her. And if I don't do something quickly they're both going to outface me and send me home in disgrace, Hope thought. Chalk up one more failure for Hope Anne Latimore. Maybe—

She snapped her fingers in Rex's ear. The big dog put on his guard dog act. One deep growl, and then the big tongue came out and he panted. Instantly all the bravado on the boy's solid face disappeared. He backed up into the doorway, pushing his sister behind him.

"That's your dog?" he asked shakily.

"That's my dog," Hope agreed. "Why don't you invite me in?"

"Yeah, why don't we?" The children backed up into the entrance hall. Hope followed right behind them.

"Your sister's name is Melody? That's nice. And you?"

"His name is Eddie," the girl piped up. "Edward, really, but he thinks that's a sort of sissy name, so Uncle Ralph said—"

"That's who I need," Hope declared, seizing on the clue. "Uncle Ralph. Did he go to Boston to work today?"

"Nope," Melody said, "he *goed* upstairs in the attic. That's where he works."

"He *goed*? He works up in the attic? Always?"

"Yup," Eddie confirmed. "Always works in the attic, he does. My sister don't speak no good English."

"And that's another—" Hope said, and then hushed. Her dad had always been a straight-arrow type. Why would he have made two such drastic errors? Uncle Ralph lived and worked here in this house, and she was supposed to stay here overnight—and even Ma had said nothing at all about that, except to bring Rex.

Bring Rex? Hope looked over her shoulder. Her gallant dog had followed her into the house, and then had immediately stretched out on the welcome mat and gone to sleep again. Some protection! A little shiver wrestled up Hope's spinal column.

Two children. She turned and studied them. The girl was pert and sassy, with enough red hair to form into a curl, topped off by a yellow ribbon. Three years old? Somebody had crammed her into a red-checked dirndl which was about a size too small, and a white blouse which was no longer as white as it might have been. A faded sort of red dirndl which matched her long curls. She was barefoot and fragile. The boy was solemnly solid, tall for eight, dressed in a pair of once blue overalls, with patches at the knees. He was barefoot as well. His hair was darker than his sister's.

Both of them had matching dark, almost black eyes, which outstared Hope without any difficulty at all.

"So I need to see your uncle," Hope said. There was a little quiver in her voice. She wasn't really sure she *did* want to see Uncle Ralph. Maybe I ought to go out and get in my car and go back to Eastport, she told herself. But then that would let Dad down, and he might yell at me, and it would let brother Michael down, and he would surely yell at me, and—

"And just who do we have here?" The deep voice came out of the dark of the hall behind the children. Hope squinted but saw little in the darkness.

"I'm Hope," she said.

"Yes, well, everybody is bound to have some," the voice said, and the man stepped forward into the edge of the light, but was still half-shadowed.

"What?"

"Hope," he said. "Everybody is bound to have some."

Eddie giggled. Hope blushed. It was a terrible pun, but she hadn't the nerve to tell him so. And then he moved forward, directly into the light.

"You!" Hope exclaimed.

"Me," he admitted. "Thought you would never meet me again, didn't you, Hope Latimore? It's been a long time since high-school days. Remember—"

"I don't care to do any remembering," Hope declared firmly. "I especially don't intend to remember you, Ralph Browne. Not after you—"

"Yes," he said, sighing. "I wasn't such a terrific success at the Graduation Prom, was I? Well, thank the Lord that we—well, I grew up. But you—you're still a tiny little thing that—"

It was her strongest passion—the one thing she hated more than anything in the world. "I am *not* a tiny little thing," she interrupted bitterly. "I *am* short, but not tiny or little. And I don't like to be—"

"Called tiny or little," he said. "Enough said. Did you hear that, kids?"

Two heads nodded.

"Being short," she continued stubbornly, "has nothing to do with intelligence, or accomplishment, or morality!"

"You could have gone all day without mentioning morality," he said. "You're a cute little—er—short thing, Miss Hope. Do you suppose you can handle these two wild Indians?"

"Without a doubt," she said stiffly, and then shuddered. The memory of her first day as a teacher in the ninth grade public school in Taunton was still strong in her mind. "A proficient and dedicated teacher," the principal had reported to the school board, "but totally unable to maintain discipline in classes of twenty-five students."

"Then in that case," Uncle Ralph said, "Eddie, you take Miss Hope's bags up to her room, and Melody, you guide her to the— And what in the Lord's name is the—"

Rex, of course. He stretched and got up, all one hundred and ten shaggy pounds of him, and wandered over to Hope. Skilled by long practice, he inserted his nose in her chilled palm, and gave a lick or two for courage's sake.

"Rex," she said pertly. "My chaperon. My mother said I couldn't stay overnight in your house without a chaperon."

"Your mother? The little—er—short lady who came by yesterday?"

"The very one," Hope retorted. "She's also a justice on the State Superior Court, you know."

"I didn't know," he said, sounding a little mournful about his own ignorance. "Your mother is a spoilsport, I suspect. Cherishes her daughter, does she? Tight rein? Home by eleven o'clock?" And then he paused while he evaluated the rest of what she had said. "The Superior Court?"

Feeling just a little superior herself, Hope added, "And my brother is a very large man with very old-fashioned ideas about his sisters."

"Good Lord. Are there more of you?"

"Yes, but they're all much bigger than me," she confessed. "And except for Michael they're all married."

"I think I'd better go back to work," he said. There was a reflective look on his face. He seemed to be thinking seriously. And then he smiled at the two children and headed for the stairs. Hope watched him go.

A slim greyhound of a man, perhaps five feet eight. In a world of tall people he was undoubtedly short; in Hope's world he was a very suitable size. Someone she had to look up to, but not one who would set her neck to aching. Well muscled. He was wearing a T-shirt that demonstrated that fact. A narrow waist, narrow hips, stuffed into blue jeans. Wide shoulders, square face and long, unruly red-blond hair. Well, now, she told herself as she watched his supple back, I *knew* there had to be some economy-sized men in the world!

He stopped at the foot of the stairs and turned around. ''Lunch at twelve,'' he announced. ''There's a computer schedule on the wall in the kitchen. Be careful about Eddie.''

And before Hope could work up a single question he was gone. Be careful about Eddie? Melody was a little doll. Now Eddie, he was a different story indeed! She looked at the watch pinned to her blouse. Three hours until lunch, if she could only figure out what lunch would be!

''Well, c'mon,'' Eddie said. He picked up her suitcase as if it were empty, and started for the stairs. Nothing romantic in that boy, Hope told herself. Big for his age, and strong, but not an ounce of romance. Now Melody made up the difference. She came over to the side opposite the dog and took Hope's hand. And promptly spoiled the scenario.

''Even my mother's bigger 'n you,'' she said as she led the way up the stairs. And then, up where the stairs made a sharp left turn, she added, ''Except you're bigger than my mom up on top. A whole lot bigger!''

Hope looked down at herself, and almost missed the next stair. She was bigger than most—well, bigger than some women her height, in the breast department, that was. She could well remember how, during her first year of teaching, high-school boys had stared and made smart remarks behind her back every time she came into a class. And how Alfred had continually tried to put his hands—

just there—until she'd given him a little judo lesson for his trouble.

"Some day you must tell me about that," Melody said.

"About what?" Eddie asked.

"About being—" Melody started to say.

"That's something your mother will explain to you," Hope said, cutting off the conversation. The last thing in the world she wanted to get into was an explanation of sexual development to an eight-year-old boy. Although she was twenty-four she was still a little embarrassed by the subject herself. And a great many other subjects dealing with the male of the species. "My mother explained it all to me when I was thirteen."

"Explained what?" Eddie insisted.

"Girl-talk," his sister said.

"This here is your room, Hope." Eddie reached for the doorknob.

"Not this one," Melody insisted. "The next one. The one with the bathroom."

Eddie shrugged, slammed the door shut and led the procession along one more door.

"That's nice," Hope said, hoping to relieve the tension that was building up in the corridor. Her own bathroom? That *was* nice. Corridor? It was a long straight hall, about as long as a narrow bowling alley, with eight or nine closed doors shutting off the light, and a small dirty window at each end. The place needs a tremendous cleaning, she told herself. It looks as if it's had a man for a housekeeper! She thanked God for the dimness; it hid her massive blush.

Eddie opened the next door down and led her into the room. He looked around at the dark brown decor, the utilitarian curtains, the plumped pillows as if he didn't believe it. "This one?" he asked his sister. She nodded. With a shrug, he dropped Hope's bag on the floor.

"C'mon," he ordered his little sister, and marched out the door and down the hall, his sibling following faithfully. Rex took a step or two in their direction, as if he was planning to join the parade.

"Rex!"

The dog stopped, looked around apologetically, and came back to her side.

"Darned dog," she muttered. Rex, totally unimpressed, circled himself a time or two and coiled up on the rug.

"So I'll unpack, take a shower, and see about lunch," Hope told herself. After all, unpacking amounted to practically nothing. She had only brought two or three sets of work clothes, four sets of undies, her vanity bag and a half-dozen pairs of socks. Taking a shower was just a shade different than swimming, and as for lunch… Sandwiches and milk? Or something like that. Kids were easy to please.

She shrugged herself out of her sweater, unbuttoned her blouse, and slipped one arm out of the sleeve. And then the noise shattered her composure. A heavy thump or two, and a massive rolling sound, pounding slowly down the length of the corridor. Melody squealed. Eddie yelled for help. Rex came up on his feet and whined at the door. Hope took a moment to recover, and then joined the procession just as the rolling thunder terminated in a massive crash. The side of the house shook.

Hope managed to get the door open, but her sleeves were so entangled that her blouse fell to the floor. And the two children were standing in front of her, holding hands.

"It was a accident," Melody stated.

"She did it," Eddie said, pointing toward the corner. Nestled up against the wall was an immensely solid bowling ball.

"Good grief." Hope sighed.

"Good grief is right." Uncle Ralph came vaulting down the stairs from the third floor. "I told you to watch out for Eddie."

"Oh, come off it," Hope snapped. "Why would a boy his age try a trick like that?"

"Well, I didn't do it," Eddie insisted. His uncle looked just the tiniest bit confused. Melody, feeling she needed a protector, moved over against Hope's leg and wrapped both hands around it.

"I din't do it," the little girl said soberly.

"Of course you didn't," Hope assured her. Two hands entwined. Two female hands, sharing God's truth.

"Well," Uncle Ralph said doubtfully, "I have work to do." He reached for the bannister and started up to the third floor. And softly, out of the range of the children's ears, he added, "And Miss Latimore, I would appreciate it if you did not appear in front of the children half-naked in future."

"What?" Hope snapped angrily. "Well, really!" She looked down at herself, blushing. She was wearing twice as much as she would have worn at any beach: a slip, a bra, a skirt— But purely by luck, she told herself. Ordinarily she would never have worn the bra. She preferred light, loose clothing, and a bra was redundant because of her well-shaped development. She glared up at him, wishing that she could make him vanish.

"Yes, well, really," he returned. A tiny smile played around his lips. "For myself, you understand, I don't object. But Eddie and Melody are—"

"Shut up!" she yelled at him. "I'm not—I'm—it was an accident!"

Two little voices giggled behind her. "I told you," Melody said. "Big, isn't she?"

Uncle Ralph was still chuckling as he went around the turn of the stairs. Hope transferred her glare to the children, whose giggles came to an abrupt halt.

She stalked back into her room and slammed the door behind her, shutting out the world and all its denizens. She dropped onto the bed, clenching her fists. "I'll quit this stupid job," she told herself. "I don't have to put up with all this—" She pounded her clenched fists on the wall. Nobody could be as angry as Hope Latimore could. "I should have given him such a knock! I should have given him such a knock ten years ago, at the dance, as well!"

A shower, she told herself. Ralph Browne! The boy who totally embarrassed me ten years ago. I could have— killed him—back then. Tearing the bodice of my dress in the middle of the dance floor! And me not wearing a slip or bra! And him laughing about it! Well, he didn't feel it was so funny after I blacked his eye for him. And then *he* explained it all to the principal as an accident, and me, I was suspended from school for a week for hitting him! Smooth-talking monster!

So I'll take a shower and change clothing. And then I'll knock him dead with a luncheon such as he's never seen before.

A good plan. She went into the bathroom, shedding clothing on the way, and turned on the hot water.

It was an old house, but the plumbing had been refurbished. There was plenty of hot water, for which she thanked the Lord. And so she rubbed and scrubbed and washed away all her anger until, a half-hour later, she had restored her calmness and climbed out of the shower.

The towels were all hanging on a hot rack. She pulled one out that seemed to be twice as big as she was, and used it to rub herself dry. Blissful. Clutching the towel in one hand, she dragged it along the floor after her as she opened the bathroom door. Three steps into the bedroom she knew she had made another terrible blunder. There was a man leaning over the foot of the bed, stripped to his boxer shorts, whistling. Uncle Ralph!

"What—?" she screeched in a voice twice as loud as the town's fire alarm. He whirled around.

"Well," he said judiciously. "Tasty. No doubt about it. But you didn't have to go to all that trouble!"

Hope seemed to be frozen in position. Not in all her years had she shared a bedroom with a man, and a naked one to boot. Well, not since she was four years old and her brother Michael was two. She managed two deep breaths.

"Get out of my bedroom," she squeaked. He grinned at her. She located the end of the towel and tried to whip it around her.

"Some mistake," he said, chuckling. "This happens to be *my* bedroom. And if you really mean to hide something you need to lift the towel a little higher."

Hope looked down. He was right. Burbling with anger, she moved the towel northward.

"Too high," he commented.

"Get-out-of-my-room," she countered as she re-adjusted the towel one more time.

"Let me repeat. You're in the wrong room."

"Y-your nephew," she stuttered.

"Yes, I can see that." He looked around the room for something. The mere fact that his eyes were off her gave some relief. Not much, just some.

"We'll argue about this later," he said. "Just as soon as I can find my pants."

With a gasp of frustration Hope retreated to the bathroom and slammed the door shut.

"I suppose that means you don't find me attractive?" The laughter in his voice penetrated the closed door. "If you plan to quit you ought to wait until after lunch," he called.

Hope doubled her fists and pounded on the door. "Go away," she yelled at the top of her voice.

"I can't until I— Ah, here they are." He came back to the door. "I couldn't just bustle out of here," he said just loudly enough to be heard through the door. "Melody is playing with her dolls in the hall, you know, and I couldn't find my pants. See you at lunch."

When she heard the bedroom door close Hope sighed in relief and sagged against the bathroom door. I *ought* to quit, she told herself. Nobody has to put up with this kind of thing. Nobody!

Weakly she dragged the door open, looked cautiously around the room, and staggered over to the bed. "I'll just wait," she muttered as she sat down, "until he makes one more smart remark, and then I'll give him such a knock he won't ever forget it!"

In the back of her mind she could hear her mother's voice. "Go ahead and quit," Mary Kate was saying. "Six different jobs in two years, but that doesn't matter. Quitting is better than punching him out. You've not grown enough to take on a full-grown man. You have to control your temper, love. Go ahead and quit. Your father might be disappointed, but he never did understand women. Go ahead, Hope."

And Hope Anne Latimore was turning red with anger and embarrassment!

"Damn! Damn! Damn!" she yelled as she beat the pillows with her tiny hands. "I won't quit, and I can't make me! And no, I won't call for help. Michael has too much to do besides nursemaiding me. I won't quit! Do you hear me, Hope Latimore? I will *not* quit!"

And since Hope Latimore was the only living soul in the bedroom at that particular moment it all made a great deal of sense. So she dried her eyes, emptied her suitcase, and managed to find something to wear. Something clean and simple and dry. A T-shirt, jeans, and sneakers.

Then she brushed her hair, which did little good. The unruly curls sprang right back into the same position as before. So she started for the kitchen. Her route took her by the wall-mounted mirror. She paused with one foot still in the air as she caught her reflection. The T-shirt molded her shape to perfection. Super-perfection. "Oh, gawd!" she muttered as she scrambled back to her suitcase and dug out a very heavy, very thick angora sweater which, when she put it on, hung loosely and limply around her trim form, and covered her like an army pup tent on a rainy day.

CHAPTER TWO

THE quiche was browning very nicely when the alarm bells went off all over the house. He had explained it but she had forgotten. The house was wired to a small computer on the wall, tucked in just behind the refrigerator. Dinner bells in this crazy house sounded like fire alarms.

Hope shuddered. She knew less than nothing about computers, despite the fact that everyone else in her family lived cheek by jowl with the things. And posted on the wall above the computer was a twenty-hour listing of everything due to happen. She had no need to consult the list, not now. Footsteps thundered from all directions. She backed off into a corner. Melody burst into the kitchen, laughing, three or four paces in front of Eddie.

"I *beatcha*, I *beatcha*," the girl caroled, dancing around her brother.

"Cheated," he muttered. "You din't—"

"Yes, I did. Liar!" The little tongue came out and wagged at him.

Uncle Ralph came in last. "Inspection," he commanded, with a voice like some dyspeptic army drill sergeant.

The two children lined up side by side like a pair of tiny soldiers, shoulders back, heads erect.

"Hands."

Two pair of hands appeared; Eddie's were palms up. Melody's were palms down.

Uncle tapped Eddie's fingertips. "Acceptable," he said authoritatively. "Only you used more water than soap." He took a sidewise step and stood before Melody.

"The other side."

Cautiously, slowly, she turned her hands over. Her palms were dark as night.

"I told ya," Eddie gloated. "She din't—"

"No comment from the ranks," Uncle Ralph commanded. "Private Melody, re-wash. Dismissed."

The little girl's lip quivered, and what looked suspiciously like tears welled in her eyes. She knuckled them away and dashed for the tiny lavatory adjacent to the kitchen. Eddie smirked and dropped into a chair.

"Uh-uh," his uncle said. "Nobody sits until the lady sits."

"Aw," the boy complained as he struggled to his feet. "It don't do no good to—"

"Any good to," his uncle corrected.

"Yeah. It don't do any good to beat her because she's always first, 'cos she's a girl! That ain't fair."

His uncle nodded sagely. "True, Eddie, but life isn't necessarily fair, you know."

Melody popped back into the kitchen, her hands dripping wet but clean. "Now," he said as he went over to hold the girl's chair. "Now for this delightful first lunch made by our new housekeeper."

"It's hot," Hope warned as she pulled the quiche pan out of the oven and placed it on the hot pad in the middle of the table. She had expected enthusiasm; she got silence.

In fact, an uneasy silence. Finally Melody climbed to her feet in the middle of her big kitchen chair and peered over the edge of the plate.

"Goll-eee," she half whispered. "What is it?"

"Quiche," Hope said. "Very Parisian. Just what you'll love."

"What's all that little green stuff?" Eddie asked. It was plain that he was not exactly overwhelmed by the presentation.

"Broccoli," Hope said firmly. "Every kid loves broccoli."

"Ugh. Not this kid."

"Me neither," said Melody.

Hope turned and stared at Uncle Ralph. He ducked his head. And grinned. Hope *knew* he was grinning, even though his face was solemn. Solemn but not sincere. Kids can't help themselves, she thought. They do what their adults do. I ought to hit him with the frying pan. Her hand stretched out unconsciously toward the top of the stove.

"Hey, I didn't say anything." His right arm came up protectively. "I eat quiche—although broccoli isn't my favorite."

"President Bush said kids didn't have to eat no broccoli," Eddie said.

"That's why he's not president any more," Hope snapped. "What is this, a junk-food family? What do you usually eat for lunch?"

"Peanut butter 'n' jelly," Melody said. "Except when Mama's cookin'."

"Mama makes nice sandwiches," Eddie contributed. "Ham, bologna, salami—stuff like that."

"And sometimes pizza," Uncle Ralph contributed. "My sister's a good cook."

So am I, Hope raged inwardly. As good as two of your sisters, if you've got that many. I ought to quit this stupid job! I ought to leave right now and never come back! I ought to—make some sandwiches!

The peanut butter, she remembered from her first kitchen inspection, was on the third shelf of the cupboard. The jelly was in the refrigerator. The bread had its own private metal box. She stalked over to the other side of the kitchen and flipped the cupboard door open. And stretched. And stretched. "Damn," she muttered under her breath. She needed another twelve inches to reach the proper shelf.

"The kitchen step-stool is by the freezer," Uncle Ralph said.

"And the Cussin' Can is next to the bread box!" Melody exclaimed.

"Of course if you were a gentleman..." Apparently he wasn't.

"And it's ten cents for every cuss word," Eddie declared.

Hope glared at all three of them. "Taxation without representation," she snapped. "That's what caused the American Revolution."

"Meanin' you don't have no money?" Eddie asked.

"No, I don't have any money," Hope snapped.

"You could always put in a IOU," Melody suggested. "That's what Uncle Ralph does. He just writes it on a piece of paper and sticks it in the can."

Yes, Hope told herself. That's what I'll do. And right after lunch I'll quit this stupid job and I'd like to see them collect on my IOU after that. Right after lunch!

"Do you always talk to yourself?" Uncle Ralph inquired. "Your lips are moving as if—"

"None of your business," Hope snapped. "I talk to myself a lot. I'm the only one who understands me."

It was hard to tell what he answered. She would have sworn it was something like, "I can believe that," but why would he be so nasty and at the same time get up and pluck the peanut butter jar off the shelf? Puzzled, she snatched up all the materials and manufactured four sandwiches. Eddie hesitated for a moment, then shrugged and bit into one. Melody acted as if Christmas had come twice this year. Uncle Ralph smiled at them all—a sort of smile that was cousin to a grimace—and cut himself a slice from the quiche.

"You don't *have* to eat that," she informed him firmly as she cut herself a rather large piece and set it on her own plate.

"Not to worry," he said. "I like quiche." And then took the daintiest bite she could possibly imagine. For a man, that was.

All of which set her off to dreaming again. For a man, that was. For his size he was a great deal of man. His shoulder muscles bulged under his thin white shirt. There was not an extra ounce of flesh anywhere from shoulders to hips. Her brother Michael was a giant of a man, having played football at Notre Dame University. Being two years older than Michael, she had spent a great deal of time looking after him, studying the male of the species, until Michael had outgrown her. Uncle Ralph was a miniature edition of Michael. Uncle Ralph?

"I don't even know what to call you," she said as she chewed.

"His name is Uncle Ralph," the little girl said.

"Browne," he said. "Ralph N. Browne. With an E."

She remembered it well, that name. She had fed it into her mind ten years before. What girl wouldn't remember the name of the boy who had stripped her half-naked on the dance floor, and had got her suspended for hitting him?

It had felt so good, she remembered, hitting him. And Michael, who hadn't been all that big in those days, had offered to beat him up—but Ma had put her foot down. And now Hope had some months with Ralph N. Browne, and she didn't know all that much about his family. There were three different Browne families in Eastport. One ran the pharmacy, the second had a small farm, and the third was—well, from the wrong side of the railroad tracks, was what people said. She wondered what Ralph N. Browne's family was like.

"You wouldn't know anyone in my family," he said. "Finished, kids?"

Eddie scrambled from his chair. "I gotta go," he said, licking at the leftover jelly on his lips.

"Wash your face," his uncle commanded.

"I gotta go," Melody said.

"Wash your face."

The two children rushed away.

"I have to go too," Uncle Ralph said as he pushed his chair back.

"Wash your face," Hope muttered.

"What?"

"I—er—said what a nice place," she substituted. He gave her a doubting look as he crumpled up his napkin and dropped it next to his plate.

"Good quiche," he said. "Make it again some time."

She nodded, wide-eyed, and watched as he left the kitchen. "Yeah, make it again," she muttered. "My life wouldn't be worth a nickel if I did! Now why would he make such a stupid statement?"

She wasn't about to find out. Not at that particular moment. A buzzer went off, activated by the computer. The dishwasher at the far end of the kitchen began to grumble. "Oh, my gawd," Hope muttered as she hurried to get the luncheon dishes into the machine without breaking them all.

Hope slammed down the lid of the machine and then walked over to confront the computer. "Damn spy," she grumbled. She made a careful check of the scheduling list taped to the wall just above the computer. A complete set of instructions for the day, it was. And within fifteen minutes she was required to be vacuuming all the downstairs rooms.

"I'm going to punch him out," she told the amused walls. "I'm going to really give it to him, and if my mother—she won't say anything. Nothing at all. She loves me."

A sharp yap from outside reminded her that she hadn't seen Rex for a month of Sundays. Well, not since that embarrassment with the bowling ball. And the shower! She thumbed her nose at the computer and dashed for the front door, where the good old dog was waiting, anxious for his lunch.

At three o'clock she was still vacuuming when the buzzer went off in the kitchen again. She raced out to check the list. "Already one hour behind schedule," she muttered. "What now?"

The computer, being one of the ignorant kind, refused to answer. She checked the list again. "Afternoon break," it said. Thank the Lord. She walked by the humming Hoover. It promptly shut itself off. She went upstairs into her room and flopped down on the bed. Then got up again to check that she was in the right room. "You'll not catch me twice with that trick," she told the door.

"No, I'll bet we can't," the deep voice behind her said.

Hope gasped and whirled around. Ralph Browne. Ralph N. Browne, to be exact. "What does the N stand for?" she asked, desperate for a chance to catch her breath.

"N is for Nothing," he said. She was leaning back against the half-opened door. He put both hands on the door, one on either side of her head, making a sort of prison out of it all. "You're a beautiful woman, Hope Latimore."

"You must be dreaming," she retorted. "Now my sister Mattie, she's beautiful."

"Ah. And you're jealous?"

"Don't be silly." Hope's face flushed and a touch of panic marked her voice. "She's gone back to Africa. Something about a railroad not working right. But I'm not jealous. How could I be jealous of my sister? Well, my stepsister, she is. And bigger than me."

"Almost anybody in the world would be bigger than you," he said, chuckling. "Eddie's eight years old and almost as tall as you are. But I'll bet nobody kisses as nicely as you." He leaned forward and down, his nose on a level with hers, his eyes staring into hers.

Green eyes, she told herself. I hadn't noticed that before. Green eyes, and he needs a shave—or maybe he's growing a beard? Nobody kisses as nicely as I do? How would he know that? I haven't done any kissing in a dog's age. Not if you don't count Becky's two children.

He was getting closer. Dangerously closer. "Rex?" she whispered. Her guard dog was asleep on the rug next to her bed. His tail thumped once, but he closed his eyes and stayed where he was. "Damn dog," she muttered.

"I can't remember when I knew a girl so set on cussing," Ralph said. He was slowly getting closer, nose touching nose by this time.

"Don't touch me," she whispered.

"Too late." His lips formed a pucker and he kissed the tip of her nose.

"I hate that," she muttered.

"I'll bet you do." He tilted his head to the right, and his lips caressed hers. There was a contact spark, almost electrical. Hope stiffened, and then relaxed. A shiver ran up her spine.

But there's nothing I can do about it, she told herself. He's bigger than I am, by almost a foot at least, and his arms— And only then did she realize that his arms were not holding her, not in the least. His hands were supporting his weight, resting on the door. Nothing was locking her in position except for the contact at her lips. And the daydream of kissing. A warm feeling, moist, hypnotic.

But he *means* to be holding me locked against him, she told herself, so there's no use fighting it, is there? And having defined her imprisonment she relaxed even further, and her arms crept up around his neck. She sighed, a gusty sigh like nothing she had ever sighed before. Her shameful lips formed to match his. Don't do that, she told herself frantically, but just saying it didn't seem to help.

There was another light touching of lips, from which *he* withdrew. And then returned to a long, deep, warm confrontation. All her senses boiled up and over. She tightened her grip on his neck; one of her feet came off the floor as she pressed against him. Like a desperate mountain climber, afraid of slipping, she burrowed into him. And might have clung for ever, but the kitchen alarms sounded, and he drew back.

"And it wasn't all my fault," Hope defended vigorously.

"No, it wasn't," he admitted. "I don't think I've been kissed like that since—well, even longer than that!"

"There's no need to boast about it!"

"I'm not boasting. That's fantastic. Do you do it that way all the time?"

"You *are* boasting. Gentlemen don't boast about— that!"

"Lust. That's what we call it, not *that*. Want to try again?"

"No, I don't. Not ever," Hope snapped. "Some people call it love, not lust."

He grinned at her. "Ah. You're in love with me?"

"Don't be silly," she said firmly. "I've been kissed before. You're not particularly good at it, if you must know." She managed to get one hand up to her mouth, and used it to scrub off the remembrance of the kiss. There was too much to scrub off.

"Tell the truth," he coaxed.

"If I did you'd be terribly embarrassed. Terribly."

He shrugged, still grinning. "Well, a guy can't win them all." The kitchen buzzers sounded again. He checked his wristwatch. "At least my scheduling is accurate, love." Before she could duck he kissed the tip of her nose again, and wheeled out into the corridor. Rex lifted one eyelid and offered a woof before going back to sleep.

"Damn dog," she muttered. "Where were you when I needed you?" Rex had nothing further to add. Hope leaned out into the corridor. Ralph was long gone. "And your schedule is in a terrible mess," she yelled down the empty hall. "Where does it say 'Time to kiss the housekeeper'?"

They all tumbled into the kitchen together at six o'clock. Hope watched them with tired eyes. The inspection was held. Rex tried to hide in the corner adjacent to the dishwasher, with not a great deal of success.

"We don't allow animals in the kitchen," Uncle Ralph declared.

"Hah!" Hope went over and patted her dog. "No dog, no cook," she announced. "No cook, no food!" And she turned up her button nose and defied him.

"What would we of had if we'd had somethin'?" Eddie asked hesitantly.

"Pizza," she said in a royal tone of voice. "Home-made pizza."

The two children sniffed the air and then turned to glare at their uncle. He tried to look them into sub-mission, with no success. "He's a very royal dog," Melody said softly, and then again, with more enthusiasm, "A very royal dog, like a king of—"

"He's got a pedigree a mile long," Eddie interrupted.

"Is that so?" Uncle Ralph mused, without looking at anyone in particular.

"On his father's side, they came over on the *Mayflower*," Hope swore. Having lied her very soul away, she then put on her heat-proof glove and opened the oven door. Lovely odors filled the kitchen from floor to ceiling.

"Lots of cheese," Melody commented.

"And linguiça," Eddie added. "Lots of linguiça."

"And there wouldn't be any leftovers," Hope said. "Rex loves pizza too."

"Black olives, red peppers, mushrooms, onions—"

"You don't have to pad the account," Ralph interrupted. "OK, the mutt—"

Both children coughed loudly. Rex got up, stretched, and came over to the table.

"Yes, the dog," Ralph corrected. "The dog is allowed in the kitchen."

A collective sigh followed Hope as she scooped out the pizza plate and placed it on the counter. "Big slices?" she asked.

"Big slices," they all agreed. Hope struggled with the heavy kitchen knife.

"If us gets it from the pizza place," Melody said, "it comes already sliced."

"But not homemade," Uncle Ralph pointed out. "Can't you cut faster?"

"''N' bigger,'' Eddie added.

Uncle Ralph inhaled deeply. "We need to buy the house a pizza cutter," he announced.

Well, Hope told herself as she put the platter on the table and stood back out of the way, at least I've done *something* right today. Ma would be proud of me!

And two mouthfuls later Ralph Browne leaned over in her direction and said, "Your mother would be proud of you."

"My mother is *always* proud of me," Hope retorted. "Is *your* mother proud of you?"

He took another huge bite out of his pizza and then, talking with his mouth stuffed, said, "You and I have to have a little talk, Miss Latimore. After the kids are in bed."

It sounded like a serious threat. Hope thought, Maybe I'd better quit this stupid job. Five years of college credits, a Master's degree, and I'm working as a housekeeper? I should quit right now, before I get involved with the "let's put the kids to bed and do the dishes" bit! I am *not* a dish-doer!

"If you don't wanna finish your pizza I could do—" Eddie started to say.

"Not fair," Melody shrieked. "That's a girl-type leftovers, and I'm the only girl, so it's mine."

"Uncle Ralph," Eddie said, sighing. "Does she *always* have to win?"

Both children were in bed by nine o'clock. Melody demanded a female-assisted bath with considerable splashing; Eddie manfully refused any kind of help. Melody had to have a story read to her; Eddie went off to bed with his Tarzan of the Apes novel. Hope supervized, but Uncle Ralph came to both rooms for a goodnight kiss.

"In the living room," he muttered as he brushed past Hope on his way downstairs. He was sitting in an old morris chair fingering his laptop computer when she finally finished the bathroom cleanup and staggered down to join him.

"So you've finally finished your first day of house-keeping," he said as he set the little computer aside.

Hope collapsed onto the couch just across from him. Her blouse was soaked, and her jeans were not much better off. She carefully folded her apron, and, finding no place to hang it, dropped it on the floor before she put her feet up.

"You didn't do too badly," he said. "For your first day, that is. But you have to keep more control over the children. Eddie is forever picking on his little sister, and needs more discipline."

"Is that the way you see it?" She put her feet back onto the floor and glared at him. "In case you can't see straight, let me tell you something. You remember the bowling ball?"

He nodded. "Eddie does that often."

"I suppose it's done often," she snapped back at him, "but it's not Eddie. I've been checking up all day. Every single fracas was started by Melody. Little Miss Butter Won't Melt in her Mouth has been terrorizing her brother—with your help, let me add—until his soul isn't his own!"

"That's a bunch of nonsense," Ralph said. He struggled out of the big morris chair and began to pace the rug, back and forth. Hope swung her feet up again to avoid being trampled.

"That sweet little girl couldn't throw that bowling ball down the corridor. It's too heavy for her."

"Yes, that's what she said. Until I caught her doing just that before supper."

"Too many justs in your sentence, not enough justice in your thought."

"Men!" she snorted. "You're all swept up in her sweet little innocence. You need a better perspective. That little girl is trampling all over you. The only one she can't fool is my dog. Rex grew old with a sweet little girl under his paw. He knows all the ropes."

"Someone we know?"

Hope blushed brick-red. "So all right. But I grew older and nicer, believe me."

"I wish I had known you better then."

"Why in the world would you have wanted to? I was a horrid little girl until I moved up to high school."

"And your brother took all the blame?"

Hope jumped to her feet. "He deserved it. Every bit of it."

"Oh? For what reason?"

"You—you wouldn't understand. He grew—"

"Too big for you?"

"Don't you dare laugh. Don't you dare!"

"Jealousy? Sibling jealousy?"

"Aagh!" Hope came to her feet and flexed her fingers at him. "You'll never understand," she snapped. "Never. All my sisters went off and married and left me all alone with Michael."

"And your mother and father?"

"Daddy was always away, and Ma—she was always busy with Michael. He's the baby, you know, and was always getting into trouble."

"In large part instituted by you?"

"Oh, shut up," she snapped. The telephone rang at her elbow. She snatched it up. "Hello?"

"Hope?" her big brother said at the other end of the line.

"Oh, Michael! It's good to hear your voice. You have no idea what—"

"I only have a minute, love. I just wanted to say that whatever you're doing down there keep doing it. Browne turned in the almost miraculous solution to our first problem at about four o'clock this afternoon. The best work he's ever done. Three or four weeks of this and we'll break through into a new construction era. Love ya." And the sound of a big wet kiss traveled down the line before the line was disconnected.

Hope stood there with the instrument in her hand, the dial tone buzzing throughout the room. Keep doing it? Three or four weeks? A very tiny tear formed in her left eye. She used a knuckle to brush at it, and missed.

"Your big brother?" Ralph asked facetiously. "The man who—"

"Oh, shut up," she muttered. "Yes, that was my big brother, and if you don't shut up I'll have him come down here right away and—"

"Teach me a lesson?"

When a large rage settles into a small body an explosion is almost inevitable. Hope looked down at the telephone dangling in her right hand. It jumped up and down, shaken by her quivering fingers. She stilled it with both hands and set it down on the end table.

"I don't need my big brother to teach you a lesson," she snarled at him. "I can do that myself!"

"Oh, you can?"

"I can." She began to stalk him; he backed away, almost stumbling over Rex. The big dog grumbled and then moved behind the couch. Ralph backed into a corner and held up both hands in a self-defense posture. Hope doubled her tiny fists.

"Easy now," he said, chuckling. "I have to work to-morrow. Your brother wouldn't like it if you injured me badly." His big grin infuriated her.

"I'll—I'll..." And now she was so angry that her shoulders shook and little spasms ran up and down her spine. "I'll teach you a lesson," she promised. She swung her right fist; he ducked back out of the way and laughed even more.

I'll teach him a lesson, Hope told herself. But I can't quit! Michael needs me *not* to quit. Mama will be disappointed if I quit after just one day. Dad will—oh, gawd!

But I *will* teach you a lesson, she promised silently. She looked up at him through the veil of her long blonde hair. The toes of her shoes were touching his. And he was laughing! With a squeal of rage she threw herself up at him, snatching at the nape of his neck with both hands, wrapping her feet around his knees, sealing off that laughter by pressing her lips down tightly on his. And the laughter was gone.

Startled, Ralph fell back against the wall and held onto her squirming body. A strange tongue hunted her mouth. The softness of her firm, full breasts pressed against him. Firm, full, wet breasts—her blouse was still dripping with bath water. His mind fumbled for some witty comment to make, found nothing to say, and no way to say it. There seemed to be only two choices: hold her tightly or let her slide through his arms and back to the floor. In typical male fashion he joined in the passion that was sweeping both of them away, and tried both methods.

It seemed like for ever, that kiss, but Hope knew better. She was no longer dangling from his neck. His arms took control, settling just below her waist and squeezing her. She kicked her dangling legs, but, curiously, her kicks only served to wind her around him even further.

He bounced her up a little higher, until she was sitting in the cup of his hands. Her lips broke away from his. She took a deep breath, stared at him close up, and put her brain back into gear.

What in the world am I doing? she asked herself frantically. There was no answer. He seemed about to impose his lips on hers again. She ducked her head until it was tucked under his chin. The warmth increased. The drowsy, comforting warmth. So when he gradually released her, and she slid down to where her feet touched the floor, she gave a little groan of protest.

His hands moved upward, away from her pert little bottom, up her sides until his thumbs touched on her breasts and then up again to tease at their swollen tips. Hope was shaken by a massive shudder—not of fear for what *he* might do next, but rather fear of what she herself might do. Never since she was thirteen had she felt such a reflex action. And that had been only a passing flash with a boy whose name she could hardly remember.

She cleared her throat nervously, and coughed. "Put me down," she commanded shakily.

"You don't plan to kill me any further?"

"No." A pause. "I don't think so."

"You *do* plan to get your brother to do it?"

"I—no, I don't think so."

"You plan to get your mother to do something?"

"No."

"You're planning to quit and run off home?"

"I—ought to, but I won't."

His hold on her relaxed. With both feet on the floor she leaned forward and rested all her weight against him.

He cradled her head between his hands and ran his fingers through her hair.

"I—have a terrible temper," she told the second button on his shirt. "Terrible."

"I didn't really notice," he said. Hope put her head back and caught a glimpse of his face. There was no laughter, no grimace, no mockery there. He looked perfectly normal, perfectly sincere.

"You're fibbing," she accused.

One of his hands dived into his pocket and came out with a massive handkerchief. He turned her slightly sidewise, and used the cloth to wipe first her eyes and then her forehead. "Am I?"

"Of course you am—are," she said gently. "Any girl could tell."

"Well, thank God you're not *any* girl," he said. "Here. Let me help you."

He shifted his grip, one hand under her legs at the knee, the other in the middle of her back, and lifted her weight off the floor and carried her over to the couch. When he sat down she slid into his lap as if it were the most natural thing to do in all the world.

Her arms went back up around the nape of his neck, and held on, gently.

"How come you're not married?" he asked.

"Me?" What an astonishing question, she thought. She searched his face as if to discover some nefarious plot. There was none to be seen. She used the knuckles on her left hand to clear the riot among her eyelashes. "Because nobody ever asked me," she answered cautiously.

"You never thought to do the asking yourself?"

"Of course not. That's not the way it's done. Besides . . ."

"Besides what?"

"I've never, ever met anybody that I've felt as if I might want to—do that with."

"Do what?"

"Oh, Lord. You know what I mean. Let me up." His arms unlocked immediately, and she staggered to her feet. "I must look a mess," she said as she readjusted her blouse, straightened her jeans, and ran a hand through her hair.

He was still sitting on the couch, unmoving. "You don't look a mess to me," he said softly.

Another massive shudder ran down her spine. "I— think I'd better go to bed." While I'm able, she thought. *Alone!* She turned and ran for the door, then up the stairs. Her faithful guardian Rex got up from behind the couch and came after her, moving as fast as his ancient legs could go.

There was a dark shadow at the far end of the upstairs hall. Hope's hand snapped on the light.

"Oh, my, I must be sleepwalking," the little girl said. Both her feet were set straddled over a massive bowling ball, her too short arms extended downward.

"With a bowling ball in your hands?" Hope queried.

"Now how did that get there?" the girl said, sitting down on the ball.

"Melody," Hope said firmly, "if that bowling ball rolls down this hall again as long as I'm here I'm going to—"

"Spank me?"

"Of course not. I don't believe in using violence against children."

"Well, that's all right, then." The girl giggled. "Get Eddie to put the ball back where it belongs, please. I can't exactly lift it.'' And the child disappeared into her own bedroom.

"The hell you can't,'' Hope Latimore said softly. "Poor Eddie. And poor Uncle Ralph as well.''

CHAPTER THREE

DAY dawned desperately on rainy Monday morning. The house was set back on the west side of the highway, tucked under the lip of a hill that seemed as if it would lock out the sun on even the best of days. On stormy days like this the old house was left in dismal shadow. Hope felt the difference of this particular day, but could not define it until some monster thundered on her door and tried to break it down. Rex snapped awake and growled. Wearily, Hope edged up on her elbows, used one hand to rub her eyes awake, and swung out of bed.

The floor was cold against her bare feet.

"There was a rug," she told her ancient dog. Rex hung his head but refused to comment. He had stolen the rug and tugged it off to just under the window, for his own comfort. And now he sat in the middle of it and whined. The door rattled again. A fist pounded.

"All right, all right," Hope growled as she fumbled for her robe. She wore one of Michael's old T-shirts for a nightgown, and an ancient green robe she had inherited from her sister Becky to cover it. The T-shirt fit her like a tent, and hung down to the tops of her toes. But it was much washed, tiredly transparent, and she dared not appear in public wearing it alone. So she struggled over to the door, still trying to tie the sash on her robe as she flipped the lock over. There was a large crowd of three standing at the door, looking as if she was responsible—for most everything.

"It's Monday," Eddie declared.

"How nice," she groaned. "A religious holiday?"

"No," Melody explained. "Only Eddie have to go to school. I don't!" The little girl sounded very proud of her own situation.

"And we have to have breakfast and Eddie needs a lunch," Uncle Ralph added. "Can't you hear the alarm bells?"

She could, but only after they had all stopped chattering. She explained all that in injured tones.

"Oh, Lord," Uncle Ralph said, sighing. "Another of those women to whom you can't talk until she's had a cup of coffee!"

"A coffee-grouch?" Eddie asked.

"But I like her," Melody insisted as she came over and hugged Hope's leg. "She's nice and she's soft, and—"

"Let me try," Eddie insisted as he came around the other side.

"And me," Uncle Ralph said.

"No, now just wait a minute," Hope said seriously. "Only girls. I don't hug men."

"But—" Eddie started to protest.

"Oh, boys I don't mind," Hope assured him quickly. "But men? Not a chance. Especially after what he did to me in high school!"

"What?" Melody prompted, all big eyes and eagerness. "What did he do?"

"He didn't do a thing," Ralph insisted. "He was found not guilty, and—"

"The jury was fixed," Hope insisted. "All men. What would you expect from a jury of men?"

"Girls," Eddie snorted, moving away from Hope. "All men is the way it ought to be."

"And if I hear any more treason like that," Hope said firmly, "there won't be any breakfast. Not today or any other day!"

"Wow," Melody said.

"Everybody down to the kitchen," Ralph Browne ordered, trying to save the day by changing the subject. And off they trooped, a clattering horde followed by a monster dog.

The panic subsided, as did the computer alarms, after a breakfast of bacon and eggs and pancakes smothered in maple syrup. Eddie went off to meet the school bus, his sack loaded with books and turkey bologna sandwiches. Melody went off upstairs to play. And Ralph Browne, his elbows on the table, sipped at his second mug of coffee. Hope, on the opposite side of the table, toyed with her own coffee mug. Fourth or fifth, perhaps. It was hard to remember. The other three had talked up a storm and she had barely pried her eyes open.

"You know very well that I didn't do a thing that night," he said.

Hope glared at him. "I know very well that you ruined my reputation that night," she said firmly. "I'll never forget. After all, it was only ten years ago. That's not something a girl forgets."

"Now be reasonable," he ordered. "We were dancing together. Doing the bunny hop, as I remember."

"And?" she asked frigidly.

"And we ran into a crowd, and somebody in that crowd had a pair of scissors and used them to cut the shoestring shoulder straps on your dress."

"Cut? Broke them, you mean. And the somebody was you, Mr. Browne. I know it was you. What are you talking about, scissors?"

"Scissors," he repeated. "And then you hit me." He rubbed the side of his cheek as if he could still recall the pain. "And knocked me down to the floor."

"For which I received a ten-day suspension from school and my mother packed me off to Attleboro to my sister Becky's house until I cooled off."

He rubbed his cheek.

"You deserved it," she muttered. "I wish I had been bigger!"

"You were big *enough*," he snapped. "There was I, the senior fullback of the high school football team, flattened by a—knee-high-to-a-grasshopper female!"

"Don't you say that," she snarled at him. "I was never knee-high to a grasshopper!" She struggled to get up from the table.

"Don't try it," he said. "Don't even think of it. You're still the same pint of peanuts, and I've grown half a foot."

Hope stopped in mid-action and stared at him. He had. It was all true. Her fingers trembled as they supported her. Not six feet five, like her brother, but five feet eight, big enough to spread destruction among Hope Latimore!

"Where," she asked hesitantly, her voice shaking, "did you get the idea about that scissor business? And how did you hide it all from the vice-principal?"

"I never had any scissors." He glowered and leaned in her direction. "And when your father came to talk to me he agreed that I didn't have the finger strength to break those shoestring things with my bare hands."

"My father?"

"Your father. And then your brother tried, and he couldn't break them either. Of course he wasn't as big then as he is now."

"*You* must have had scissors—or a knife," she said firmly. "But why would you want to do such a thing?"

"I had no reason, and I had neither scissors nor knife," he said. "I liked you. A lot. And then you transferred to the Catholic high school, and that was the end of that romance!''

"But..." The anger rose again, bringing a red flush to her cheek. Always the left cheek. It was ridiculous. And she had liked him a lot in those days too. More than she could say. But two years under the thumb of the Sisters of Mercy had taken care of *that* delusion.

"I almost became a nun," she muttered. "All because of you! Who else would want to embarrass me like that?"

"Sophie Winters," he said promptly. "She was jealous."

"But—but—Sophie wouldn't do a thing like that! That's not possible. We were good friends—but of course she left Eastport just after—"

"Yes," he agreed. "And she was dancing with Ratty Flannigan that night. And she gave him her scissors and laughed about it. I heard them talking about it the next day."

"Ratty Flannigan? I barely knew him. A big guy. What happened to—?"

"Two days after the dance I beat the hell out of him. He could have killed you with those scissors."

"But he was so big..."

"Size doesn't count. It's skill that counts."

"I don't know—"

"I know. You still don't believe it. Your mother told me that. I always liked your mother." He shoved his chair away from the table and stomped down the hall. Halfway back to his attic studio he must have met Melody. Hope could hear them laughing together.

"Me too," she muttered. "I always liked my mother!"

But the laughter reminded her. There was something that needed doing, and she could get even at the same time. She called Melody out to the kitchen and explained.

"Dress?" the little girl asked in surprise. "I already got a dress."

"Yes, but it doesn't fit right," Hope explained, "and the color is all wrong for a girl with red hair, and you've grown a whole bunch since your mother bought it for you."

"My mother didn't bought it for me," Melody explained patiently. "Uncle Ralph *buyed* it for me for my birthday. Ain't he a nice uncle?"

Watch your step, Hope warned herself. One convincing remark and we could have Uncle Ralph hanging from the yard-arm!

"But you're ever so much bigger now," she said sweetly. "Why, Uncle Ralph would be pleased as punch to buy you another one—maybe two. You deserve at least two. You're a beautiful girl."

"Are I?" Melody scrambled for a chair and peered into the wall mirror.

"You are," Hope assured her. "Let's go brush your hair and then we'll go tell Uncle Ralph what a lucky man he is."

But Uncle Ralph appeared to have a different opinion. He turned away from his work table with a glare on his face. "I don't like to be interrupted," he thundered at them. "My work—"

"Surely your work isn't as important as your niece," Hope objected. "She's heartbroken. Her only dress is almost old as she is. I can take her down to the Galleria Mall and outfit her for the future. Next year she'll be in kindergarten. You wouldn't want to shame the girl, would you? All you'd have to do is sign the check. Or perhaps you'd rather let us use your credit card? I'm sure you have one."

"Dear God," he muttered. "I'm being mugged in my own home!"

Which gave Hope another idea. "We could go now, and have lunch in the restaurant at the Mall. I could leave you some sandwiches for your lunch, and we would be away until Eddie comes home, and you could have all that marvelous loneliness in which to work." She paused to catch her breath.

"All right," he muttered. "Go. Spend. She's a girl; we might as well bring her up in the American tradition." One-handed, he flipped his wallet from his back pocket, fingered out a gold Visa card, and spun it over to Hope. "Go," he muttered as he turned back to his keyboard. Hope grabbed Melody's hand, winked at her, and hustled them both down the stairs. Behind them Hope could hear his mumbling as he tried to remember just where he was in his intricate puzzle.

"I don't know about cards," the little girl said querulously as they reached the next landing. "Is that enough to buy two dresses?"

"I would think so," Hope replied cautiously. "It has a five-thousand-dollar credit limit. Maybe even three dresses!"

"My gracious," Melody crowed. "What a nice uncle!"

"What a nice uncle indeed," Hope agreed amiably, then washed faces and hands, changed the tot's training pants, and led the way to the door.

"Gotta run," the child said as the rain pummeled her face.

"No need," Hope insisted, using a finger to test the weight of the rain. "I'll bring my Jeep around."

"You gotta Jeep? Uncle Ralph has a Buick and a truck."

"Lucky Uncle Ralph." Hope buttoned up her raincoat. Rex, willing to join any expedition, had to be shooed back into the house. He went, disgruntled. "And you stay on the porch, girl."

"Or else you'll yell at me?"

"Or else I might run over you. I'm a terrible driver. Stay on the porch."

Melody stuck her thumb in her mouth, as if she always did what she was told.

Hope dashed for her car, parked about twenty feet from the side of the house. The old Jeep sputtered, coughed, and started with a roar. The rain had manufactured a small mud slide against the side of the house, but the Jeep's four-wheel drive locked onto a safe passage. She slid to a stop against the second stair of the porch, and pushed the side door open. Melody came prancing down and into the shelter of the car. Before Hope could secure the door Rex came bounding out of the house and squeezed his way into the back seat.

"Doggie needs a dress too?"

"Hardly. Doggie is in a lot of trouble. They don't allow dogs at the Galleria Mall!"

"But they do allow girls?"

"Of course they do, silly. Fasten your seat belt. Massachusetts State law requires everybody to wear a belt—especially little girls."

"I are not a *little* girl." The thumb went back into her mouth.

"Of course you are not. You're a big girl. Rex! Get down off the seat!"

With her party assembled, Hope shifted gears and started out sedately for Route 138 South. There was not a great deal of traffic. Most of the Boston commuters had headed north long ago.

As little traffic as there was, Melody spotted it, chattered about it, and squirmed in her seat to search for more. They drove the bypass around Taunton, came out the other side, crossed the railroad tracks, and zoomed up into the Mall parking lot.

"Big," Melody commented.

"Biggest in southern Massachusetts," Hope assured her. "And full. And you remind me. We have to get you a children's car seat."

"Uncle Ralph have got one," the child remarked. "I don't like it. I won't sit in no kid's seat, so don't buy one."

"See that policeman over there?"

"Yeah."

"If I don't get a child seat they're going to arrest me and throw me in jail."

"I don't care." Accompanied by a sullen shrug.

Think quickly, Hope Latimore! "And then they'll take you home and arrest your uncle Ralph and throw *him* in jail as well!"

"Oh, my! They can't do that!"

"How true." Hope sighed. Female fraternization had just broken into a thousand pieces. "Come on, love, let's go."

So they left Rex to guard the Jeep, under the threat of the Death of a Thousand Cuts, and went off as fast as they could go to the nearest doors. The dog paid little attention. He obviously thought Hope had said the Death of a Thousand Cats, and there was really nothing better that the big old dog might like than a thousand—or ten thousand—cats to annoy.

Three hours, six dresses, three pairs of shoes and a lunch later, they had combed Bradleys, Mother's Care, Gap for Kids, Sears, and Penny's, and were marching on Filene's with underwear in mind when an unwary saleswoman said, "And just what will the baby prefer?" And then added insult to injury by trying to pat Melody on the head.

The child stopped, planted both feet in the middle of the aisle, and yelled, "I ain't no baby!" Hope had to shrug herself back into her skin. Melody had the loudest young voice in all of New England. And to emphasize her slight displeasure she plumped herself down on the floor and began to roar. The saleswoman backed off a step or two for self-protection.

Hope's face turned blush-red. "Tired," she tried to explain. "She needs her nap."

Melody snarled at her. Half a dozen adjacent mothers nodded and advised. A tall, tired floor-walker could be seen heading in the direction of the noise. Hope looked around desperately. There seemed to be only one way out of the dilemma: snatch the child up and run for the door.

Unfortunately the floor-walker was a gentle sort of man. He bent down toward Melody. "I have a half-dozen grandchildren," he said, "and I know all about—"

"I wouldn't recommend that you..." Hope began.

And the cute little baby girl sitting on the floor smiled up at him—and bit his finger.

The elderly gentleman said several words in what seemed to be a foreign language. He straightened up. "And in addition," he said, with a great deal of dignity which somehow failed to match his formerly friendly face, "your child has wet itself!"

"Herself," Hope corrected.

"Nevertheless—"

"If you hadn't all yelled so much at her..." Hope said desperately. "She's only a—" And then she stopped. One more usage of the "Baby" word would turn the world upside down. Melody stopped crying; her dark eyes tracked Hope, who was jittering back and forth, not knowing what to do next.

"Madam?" the man prompted.

Hope threw up her hands in defeat. "Sh-she's not my child," she stammered. "She—" The audience hissed.

"Mama," Melody said as she struggled to her feet. "I wetted myself!"

Hope snatched at the child's hand. In the distance she could see the uniformed security officer moving in their direction, along with a dozen or more know-it-alls and curiosity seekers. There was only one thing to do: duck behind the big dress racks. Which they did.

It worked well for a few minutes; Hope followed the conversation. And then a hateful tall voice said, "Over there."

Melody tried to say something. Hope shushed her with a finger. The girl grinned at her and pointed. Not wanting to look, Hope did. A pair of black male shoes were standing close to her. "Over here," the tall voice announced. Hope followed her eyes up and up to where his mouth was.

"Oh, my gawd," she muttered. "Why did you have to squeal on us?"

The man reached down and patted her head as she struggled to stand up.

Melody took her thumb out of her mouth. "Big," she said.

Hope nodded. "Alfred Pleasanton," she said grimly.

"You got me fired from my job with Latimore Incorporated," he said pleasantly. "Tit for tat."

Hope knew exactly what he meant. She had gone to a tough school, and he didn't have any interest at all in tat. "From me you'll never get any—" Hope snorted, and stopped talking before she put her foot in her mouth. And besides, the security policeman had finally caught up with her.

*   *   *

Ralph Browne sat in the big morris chair, cuddling the nightgown-clad Melody in his lap. Eddie sat on the floor by his feet, leaning against Rex. Hope sat across from them on the couch, wishing that the interrogation were over.

"And then what happened?" Uncle Ralph persisted.

"Then she grabbed my hand," the child said, "and tried to pick me up, but I was too slipp'ry, and the policeman was coming, so she pulled me behind the dress racks and we stooped down and hided—"

"Hid," Eddie contributed.

"How old is this kid, anyway?" Hope asked wearily, still tasting the bitterness of a plan gone massively awry. "Three going on thirty?"

"Not exactly," Ralph said. "She's a sweet little thing, three years old. But a week ago she was only two. And her mother has been ill for over six months, and—"

Eddie sidled over toward Hope and whispered in her ear, "She ain't really potty-trained."

"And then they 'rested her for child somethin' and took us to the police station," Melody chattered on.

"Let Hope tell it."

"So they tried to charge me with child abandonment," Hope grumbled. "And I don't even *have* a child!"

"And they gived me a ice-cream cone," Melody finished gleefully.

"And so you called your father?"

"Me? Call my father? I'm not *that* brave. I called my mother, that's who."

"Who *comed* and rescued us," Melody concluded. "Nice lady. I like your mother, Hope. 'N' she has this big car and there's a little TV in the back 'n' everything and she drived us back here to the house 'n' she was laughin' all the way from the police station to the house. And what do you think about that?''

''Boy, Hope, was you taken,'' Eddie said. ''I'm sorry about all that. I wouldn't want you to leave. You're nice.''

''Thank you,'' Hope said. ''Somewhere along the line I have this feeling that I was being conned by—''

''By a tiny *con person* whom we all know,'' Uncle Ralph said. ''Eddie, why don't you go upstairs and have your bath?''

The boy got up slowly, came by to give Hope a kiss on her cheek, and started for the door. ''I ain't never gonna get married,'' the boy said morosely as he went out and up the stairs.

''Me neither,'' Hope said glumly. The three of them sat and looked at each other. Rex got up and came over to Hope, dropping his massive head on her lap. A slurp or two from his heavy wet tongue offered a little compassion.

''Now then,'' Uncle Ralph said, ''Melody, you hop upstairs to bed and after I talk for a minute with Hope I'll come up and tuck you in.''

''I'd rather have Hope to tuck me in—and read a story?''

''I could read you a story,'' Ralph said in an injured tone. ''Don't you remember? I used to read you a story every week.''

''You's a nice uncle,'' the girl responded, shaking her head, ''but Hope have much better stories, and—''

''Go along now,'' Hope coaxed. ''I'll come as soon as I'm finished with your nice uncle.''

Melody slipped off her uncle's lap, offered him a kiss, gave Rex a pat, and then administered an enthusiastic hug to Hope. ''Ain't we havin' a *wonnerful* day?'' Her face was lit from ear to ear. *"Magnifersunt!"* And she ran out of the room.

"Well, it certainly looks as if you've stolen my little girl," Ralph said solemnly.

"Why didn't you tell me?" she asked, exasperated. "She was wearing training pants. I thought surely she was—"

"I'm afraid not, and it just slipped my mind."

"Nonsense. It's all cupboard love. Now, tell me some more about her."

"Her who?"

"Melody's mother."

"There's not much to say. Her mother has been sick off and on for a lot of the little tyke's life."

"So that's why she's always nagging her brother. The bowling-ball act, and things like that."

"She's looking for attention."

"No, not attention. She's looking for love."

"Oh? You studied psychology at the university?"

"Who, me?"

"Of course you."

"No, I was an English major. I studied psychology in the kitchen with my mother. Along with baking and cooking and—"

"You're trying to tell me something about your mother?"

"No..." She hesitated, debating. "No, I'm not trying to tell you anything about my mother."

"Then about you?"

"Why don't you leave me alone?" Hope blurted. "I—don't need any analysis. Especially from a man like you!"

"Dear heaven, you're not still holding all that high-school business over my head, are you?" He got up from his chair and stalked across the room. Hope vaulted to her feet and dashed behind the couch for protection.

"Don't you *dare* lay a finger on me," she threatened.

"Finger?" He laughed, a low, masculine laugh that sent little shivers up and down Hope's spine.

There were some things her mother had told her about men, but it was all... theoretical—or at least so it had seemed at the time. But there was one thing her mother had never mentioned. This adult male facing her seemed to be reading her mind!

He took another step or two in her direction. "Scared, Hope?"

"Not of you," she returned, biting on her tongue. "Alfred, maybe, or people like him. Certainly not you!"

He came to a quick stop. "Alfred?"

"Not somebody you'd know," she murmured. "Not somebody you would want to know."

"Maybe you'd better tell me about Alfred."

"Maybe I'd better not."

"Hmm." He turned away from the couch and walked over to the drinks cabinet. "I'm having a brandy. Would you like something?"

"No—I'd better go upstairs and see to Melody."

"You could have a drink with me first," he insisted as he opened the refrigerator section of the cabinet. "Orange juice?"

So what could be dangerous about a little sip of orange juice? she asked herself. Ralph really is a nice man—after a fashion, I suppose. "Yes, I'll have an orange juice," she said, doing her best to suppress all the little quaverings in her voice.

He was half-buried in the shadows, and she missed all the nuances—the sparkle in his eyes, the small curved grin that tugged at the corners of his mouth. He half filled a glass for her and came back to the couch.

"I don't understand," he mused, "why I've lost control over my favorite niece. What do you suppose it is?"

Hope shrugged. "Wrong sex, I suppose."

"Ah. That's a low blow for which there is no cure," he said. She could hear the little chuckle behind his words. "So we'll drink a toast."

"A toast? To what, for goodness' sake?"

"Are you sure your mother told you everything you need to know in life?"

"Of course she did." The ice in Hope's drink rattled. "A toast to what?"

He grinned at her, a wide, deep grin, of the sort the Wolf used on Little Red Riding Hood. "Why, to the *right* sex, my dear."

Oh, my, Hope thought as she missed her mouth and almost drowned herself in orange juice. I *hope* my mother told me everything I *ought* to know. Using both hands, she set the glass down on the large wide arm of the couch.

"I think I'll go up to Melody now," she mumbled, and fled from the scene.

The upper floor was dim. The storm which had drenched the east coast was still beating at the windows. Eddie was fast asleep, with his reading lamp clamped to the head of his bed. Hope stole quietly into his room, re-arranged his blankets, and turned off his lamp. In the semidarkness he no longer looked eight years old. His face had softened, and his eyes blinked a time or two; his book was clutched between both hands. He almost looked the twin of his sister. Hope gently tugged the book away, and leaned over to kiss his forehead. "Goodnight," she whispered. One of his eyes popped open, and then shut again.

"G'night, Mama," he returned, and rolled over on his side.

What a nice thing to say, Hope told herself. It must be nice to be somebody's mother. She tucked both his hands back under the duvet, admired him for a moment, and then tiptoed out of the room.

Melody was a different story indeed. She was asleep, but evidently had thrashed and turned and rolled until she was almost smothered by her blankets. Hope gently unwound her and then found her hairbrush. The child's long hair was coiled around her shoulders; her body was sprawled out in an unrestrained fashion and her cheeks were twitching, as if she was involved in a long and unpleasant dream.

Gentle strokes with the hairbrush, gentle care, and some degree of order was restored. She looked like some well-fashioned doll, wrapped in her white flannel nightgown. Hope restored her blankets, and kissed her forehead before stealing out. The night light, always kept on, guided her out the door.

She progressed down the hall to her own room, where Rex was a dark shadow standing guard in front of the door, and the sheets on her bed were as cold as the Hetland ice-skating rink. She shivered as she changed into her brother's T-shirt, and made herself a little cave under the blankets.

There was a great deal of noise from outside. The glass in one of her bedroom windows was loose. It rattled as the storm attacked. Occasionally a car streaked down Route 138, its whirring tires singing a little song. Funny, she thought, they all seem to drive faster as the night grows darker—as if they're all hurrying home to their—to their what? Loved ones?

A little flicker of loneliness swirled around her room and buried itself in her heart. A couple of miles away

from the Latimore home and already she was—damn!
The truth caught up with her without warning. Not
lonely for Ma and Pa and Michael, although she loved
them all most dearly. Not at all. Lonely for that man
she had left downstairs in the living room. Lonely for
Ralph Browne. And that *really* startled her. Lonely for
that—man! The bane of her youthful days. Lonely for—

Her bedroom door squeaked as it opened. Rex,
crowded out of his favorite spot on the floor by her bed,
grumbled as he shifted his position. Hope froze, legs
stretched tensely flat and tight against her body, arms
above the blankets, fists clenched. Would he *dare* to
break into her bedroom? Would he have the colossal
nerve to climb into her bed and—do whatever it was that
men did? Her mattress sagged.

A warm body nestled up against her, scrambled for a
comfortable position, and tossed an arm across Hope's
shoulder.

"Hope," little Melody muttered. "There's a dragon
at my window. He's tryin' to bust in and eat me. I
scared."

Hope fell all the way down the side of her world. *He*
didn't have the nerve to come. Was she glad—or not?

"That's all right, love," she comforted. "Stay with
me. No dragons can get us in here." She pulled the little
body closer, smoothed the child's hair, and resumed
breathing. A little disappointed breathing, to be truthful.
But what would she have done if it *had* been Uncle
Ralph? She had no answer, so she squirmed an inch or
two to the side of the bed to make some room for herself,
and eventually fell asleep.

Some time during the night the temperature began to
drop. The wind no longer rattled; now it howled, like a
disappointed hunter trying to break in. The child
quivered and woke her up.

At midnight she managed to carry the little girl back to her own bed, where she settled her and smoothed her blankets and quilts. Melody was restless. Hope gently sang her a calming song, then sat in the rocking chair and used one foot to swing herself back and forth. The chair squeaked, and did more to put the girl back to sleep than all the songs in the world could have done.

By one-thirty the storm outside had risen another decibel or two and the furnace kept clicking on and off in a losing battle with the falling temperature. Hope made one more quiet check of both the children and went back to her own room.

The floor was cold, her sheets were half-frozen, and Rex had struggled up onto her bed. "Get down, monster," she muttered, and then dived into the warm little nest that her dog had created. Her conscience bothered her, but not for very long.

An hour later Melody came down the hall again, tugging her favorite rag doll by its leg. "I cold," the child said, and climbed up into Hope's bed again without leave. Both her ice-cold feet came up against Hope's warm bottom, and shocked her awake. Another half an hour was required to settle things down again.

As she dropped off, Hope Latimore entered a delightful dream. Ralph Browne was anchored to a red buoy, some twenty feet offshore at Plymouth, in a winter storm. The buoy was tied up to the wharf by a two-inch-thick Manila rope. And Hope was standing on the wharf with a sharp knife, with which she was whittling the end of the rope, an inch at a time. It was immensely enjoyable, until a rogue wave smashed over the wharf and ruined everything. "Hope," the wave said. "Hope?"

CHAPTER FOUR

BY FOUR in the morning the rain had ceased, and then the snow came. And not one of those slow, gentle snowstorms, although it started that way. This one rang all the alarm bells in weather stations from the borders of Massachusetts to the Great Lakes. At five in the morning only a few wet flakes were drifting down. By six the cold wind had risen to gale force. "The Montreal Express", the local radio station mourned. A blizzard whirled down out of Canada, stomping across New England like a prehistoric monster, dumping off carloads of the white stuff indiscriminately.

Eddie came to Hope's room at six-thirty, pulling back the curtains on her windows to be sure she could see. He jumped into the warm bed and nudged Melody awake. "G'wan," the little girl grumbled. "You hafta go to school."

"Ain't gonna be any school," the boy insisted. "Is there, Hope?"

Hope managed a sigh, sat up in bed and opened one eye. Immediately she could feel the tendrils of the storm leaking through the windowsills. "What's this?" she grumbled. "Now I'm in charge of 'no school' calls? That's your uncle's job. Go ask him what—"

"I did," Eddie interrupted.

"And he said?"

"'Go ask Hope,' is what he said. 'She's in charge of the house,' he said. So what do you think, Hope?"

"I'll kill that man," she muttered. "They'll find his body in the springtime long after the snow melts!"

"That's scary," Melody shivered. "Uncle Ralph is the *nicest* uncle in the family."

"Humph," Eddie snorted. "He's the *only* uncle in the family."

"All right. Don't yell," Hope said. "I'm going to have a headache. I *know* I'm going to. I can feel it coming."

"Well, before it comes," practical Eddie coaxed, "why don't you just say that the schools are closed?"

"The schools are closed," Hope mumbled, and then fell backward into the warmth of the blankets, both eyes closed.

"That's not fair," Melody complained.

"What's not fair?"

"I don't got no school, so I don't got no school closin', but Eddie, he's got a school an' now it's closed. That's not sharing. You gotta go tell Uncle Ralph."

"I wouldn't do that," Eddie warned.

"She has to," Melody insisted.

"All right; before there's a fight, I'll go tell Uncle Ralph," Hope muttered. She managed to sit back up, but opening an eye was beyond her.

"I wouldn't do that if I was you," Eddie insisted.

"Look, I'm going," Hope said, sighing. She sidled out of the warmth, picked up her robe, and headed for the door.

"I wouldn't do that," Eddie said again, but by that time Hope was out the door, still with both eyes closed, fumbling for the light switch in the corridor.

"She's gotta go," Melody insisted.

"She's already gone," Eddie retorted. "She'll be sorry."

"Why?"

"'Cos Uncle Ralph, he don't sleep with no pajamas," Eddie mumbled as he moved into the recently vacated warm spot in the bed and closed his eyes.

* * *

Not knowing as much as children do, Hope used one hand to feel her way down the hall, both eyes still closed. Ralph's room was the last on the left. A suite, in fact, with its own attached bathroom, and enough space for his table and a small computer. His door was half-open. "So I can hear the kids," he had explained on her first day in the house. It made a simple sort of sense to Hope Latimore. In fact, it boosted his "nice" rating a few slots higher than before. Not *very* high, but certainly higher than she had known from her high-school days.

"Ralph," she whispered as her cold feet hesitated just over the threshold. There was no answer. She allowed her feet a couple more steps into the depth of the room; her extended right hand made contact with the foot of his bed. "Ralph?" No answer.

Navigating with one hand and only one eye half-open, she rounded the corner of the bed. All the curtains were drawn. The room was as dark as the ace of spades. And her searching fingers indicated that the bed was empty.

"Ralph," she muttered angrily. He couldn't have been gone long. The sheets were still warm, and her feet were painfully cold. The wind howled outside the near window, destroying the shower noises from his bathroom.

"Hell and damnation," Hope Latimore muttered as she fell back on the bed, shoved her feet into the warmest section available, and shrugged his blankets up almost over her head. "I'll ask him when he comes back." And the smallest member of the Latimore family was asleep before she even thought about analyzing her position.

The wind strengthened. The bed rocked and then settled back. Dimly aware, Hope held onto the edge of the bed and nestled deeper into her cocoon. The heat doubled; Melody, Hope told herself as her feet touched warm flesh. She settled back contentedly and soon was deep in sleep. And then the bell went off just at her ear.

She could only spare one eye. The other was still under the blankets. The room was lighter and brighter than she remembered. The telephone on top of the bedside table, just by her nose, rang again. She tried to sit up, but something held her down. She moved her head, just enough to see what was locking her in place. A hand with arm attached. A thick bronzed arm, disappearing under the blankets. The hand was attached firmly to her left breast. A large masculine hand. She was still too deep in sleep to be alarmed.

A body's weight pressed her down into the mattress as another arm appeared over her head and picked up the telephone.

"Who?" There was a moment's pause. "Yes, she's here." A finger tapped on her shoulder. "It's for you."

"For me? Who?" Hope muttered groggily. "Tell him to call back next Tuesday."

"It's a her," Uncle Ralph said distinctly. "She wouldn't like it if you—"

"Get off my back," Hope muttered. "Tell her there's no school. It's snowing too hard."

"I don't believe this—"

"Shut up," Hope interrupted as she dived back under the covers.

He said something softly into the telephone and then dropped it back on its cradle.

A twinge of awareness swept over Hope. "Who was it?" she asked as he rolled his heavy weight off her. His heavy weight? A very nasty suspicion began to grow in a corner of her sleepy mind. Dreams didn't have weight! "Who?"

"Well, she *said* she was your mother."

"She *said*?" Hope snapped up out of her cocoon, startled.

"I wouldn't know. I've never had a telephone call from your mother before!"

"What—?" She extended one leg in the opposite direction and touched on another thigh. Too large to be one of the children's. And the voice didn't match. Her toes were touching bare skin, no matter how high she raised her foot. She snatched it back. "What did you tell her?" she demanded.

"That you were hiding under the bedcovers and wouldn't come up for air."

"What—what bedcovers?"

"These—right under my elbow."

Hope sat up straight, knocking his hand loose from its precarious position on her breast. "You told my *mother* that I was—"

"Well, I didn't tell her everything, you know. I'm not that stupid."

She bundled all the blankets around her. *He* was naked, and in her worn T-shirt she was as good as. Go on the offensive, woman, she commanded herself, shivering. "What are you doing in my bed?" she asked angrily. Shouted, in fact.

"You have the poorest sense of direction of any woman I've ever met." He tugged back his share of the blankets and settled back on his pillow. But that left one of his hands to rest on her hip, which the rumpled T-shirt no longer covered. She shifted her position and glared at him. "As it happens, this is *my* bed!"

Hope groaned. Either this was another major nightmare in her short life or the movement of his hand on her hip was dislodging more than her T-shirt. "Stop that!"

"Sure. Stop what?"

"Stop what you're doing!"

"Oh, certainly." But they were only words; his hand kept moving.

"Damn you."

"So I'm not the one who snuck down the hall and climbed into my bed."

"Snuck?" she shrieked.

"Snuck. Sneaked? I never was much good with grammar. And why else would you come all this distance if not for a little sex? Relax. There's no better way to start off a snowy day."

"That's it," she snarled. "I came all this way to ask you if Eddie had to go to school, and I stopped for just a second to warm my feet in your empty bed, and you immediately assaulted me! What kind of a man are you?"

"Oh, the usual kind," he said as he leaned over to her side of the bed and smiled down at her. "You know. Storm, rape, pillage and all that."

"No, I don't know," she snapped as she rolled away from the bed and slammed down onto the cold linoleum. "And I don't want to find out!" The fall hurt. She said a few words she had learned at one of the construction sites.

"No sense working up a bad temper," he said, chuckling. "There's more snow out there than you could shake a stick at. You couldn't possibly run home to your mother on a day like this. Those drifts would be up to your—well, probably higher than that!"

"You are—some sort of monster," she snarled at him. "You—"

"Look," Melody said from the half-opened door.

"I'm lookin'," Eddie said from just behind her. "Just like Mommy and Dad. Are you two gonna get married, Uncle Ralph?"

"That will be a cold day in winter!" Hope was struggling to get herself covered by her disarranged T-shirt.

"I don't think the lady is interested at the moment," Uncle Ralph said, sighing. "It would be fun."

"Don't kid yourself," Hope retorted. "You wouldn't like it at all. Not at all!" She struggled to her feet. Rex managed to squirm between the children and came to her. At least the old dog was warm—and big enough to help with her coverage. She patted his ancient head and pulled him closer.

"Well, if you ain't going to get married today I don't think I should have to go to school," Eddie commented. "The snow must be ten feet deep by now."

"Hardly," his uncle said. "But no, you don't have to go to school. Now, would the pack of you go away and let me sleep? I've been up half the night with a sick computer. Back to bed, everybody."

"What a good idea," Hope contributed. Both of her eyes had popped open on their own account, but she still needed a lot of sleep or a half-dozen cups of coffee.

"But I'm hungry," Melody complained.

Hope stared at the little girl. She was standing there, feet apart, trying to work up a few tears. It was something that Hope knew all about. She had been that kind of little monster years ago herself.

"Come on, little tyke. Let's go down to the kitchen." Eddie grabbed at his sister's hand. "Me too?"

"So scrambled eggs, sausages, toast and orange juice," Hope announced as she turned around. Rex panted at her. "And dog biscuits," she added.

"You know somethin'?" Eddie asked. "You been here two days now, and we ain't had no oatmeal at all."

"Oh?" Hope stopped, shifted into neutral, and looked at them both suspiciously. "You like oatmeal?"

"Hate it," the boy responded. "But that's all Uncle Ralph knows how to cook."

"Love Uncle Ralph," Melody chirped.

"But hate oatmeal?"

"So why *don't* you marry Uncle Ralph?" Eddie questioned. "Sometimes when Mommy gets mad at Daddy she yells at him, and says 'Don't tell me about my brother. I wish he were married and then you'd find out what kind of saint he is!' What does that mean?"

"I don't know," Hope responded cautiously as she puttered around the stove. "I haven't any idea. I've never been married. One sausage or two?"

Rex barked three times. The children both nodded in agreement. Hope Latimore shrugged and set about the business of being a provider. Eventually silence settled over the busy kitchen; the snow continued.

Hope settled for a piece of toast and a glass of orange juice as she watched Melody and Eddie and Rex settle into their breakfasts. Cute kids, she thought. Why don't I marry their uncle and have some cute kids of my own? Because I haven't been asked? Because he has a bad track record? Because he might just be too smart for a girl like me? A shudder ran up and down her spine. Raised in a family of near-geniuses, dumb enough to hold last place in the race for life? What could Ralph's sister have meant by that "what kind of a saint he is"? That he isn't a saint at all?

Of course I could marry him and reform him. A good woman can always do that—can't she? Or can she?

This was one of the million subjects discussed by her married sisters and her mother. And the conclusion always drawn?

"Not on your life," Ma always preached. "You have to take him as God made him or not take him at all."

At which her sister Becky would break down in laughter. "In which case none of us would ever get married at all—"

"But you can always change yourself," Mattie would interject softly, and the conversation would switch back to recipes, memories and religion.

And that's a thought to think about, Hope told herself. You can always change yourself. Now, about Ralph . . . !

And at that point the bull of the Browne family stomped into the kitchen and glared at them all.

"Everybody but me gets breakfast?"

"Yes."

"Who said that?"

"She did," Melody said, pointing to Hope.

"She did," Eddie said, pointing to Melody.

"Beats me," Hope said. "Did you want something?"

"Of course I want something," he grumbled.

"Oatmeal?"

"Oatmeal? I hate oatmeal!" He slammed himself down into the chair between Melody and Eddie. "If I wanted oatmeal I could make it for myself."

"I'm glad to hear that," Hope said formally. "After this morning's episode I don't plan to make anything for you. Ever."

Melody tugged at her brother's sleeve. "What's that mean—*episode*?" she whispered.

"I dunno," her brother admitted. "We don't have that word in my grade."

"Uncle Ralph?"

"I—ah—don't have that in my grade either," he muttered. "It has something to do with TV programs—you know, they show you a program on Saturday but you don't see the next part of it until the next Saturday."

"Coward," Hope snapped at him, and then ducked her head. She hadn't meant for either of the children to hear. She dabbed at her eye and then smiled at the children. "Now you two get upstairs and wash; and then you can get dressed. Something warm and comfortable. Maybe if it's not too cold we can—you and your uncle can—go out in the snow for a few minutes."

"Hey—" Uncle Ralph started to say.

"Hey, great," Eddie yelled.

"But—" Uncle Ralph began to protest.

"But you have to go out and shovel the driveway anyway," Hope interrupted sweetly. "In case of fire, or something like that. Eddie is almost a man. He could help you. Melody, I'm afraid, is too short for this storm. Maybe you could help me, darling. I'm going to make some homemade bread for us. Isn't that a good idea, Uncle Ralph?"

"Great idea," he said heartily. But as he passed Hope's chair he gripped her shoulder in not too gentle a grasp. "I am not," he whispered fiercely in her ear as he bent over her, "*your* uncle!" After which he kissed her gently on her blush-red cheek and swaggered out of the kitchen, with Eddie racing along behind him.

"I could break his head," she muttered as the males of the species departed.

"Break his head?" Melody protested. "Good ole Uncle Ralph?"

"His bread," Hope said. "Bake his bread."

"Oh." The little girl slid out of her chair. "C'mon. I never baked no bread before."

The kitchen work was pleasant and orderly. "An that's going to be bread?" Melody had followed all the directions, but with a considerable amount of doubt.

"That's going to be bread," Hope assured her. "Have faith. You are about to see a miracle of chemistry."

"I are?"

"You are. Beat up on that dough as hard as you can."

The beating up was fine, but eventually the dough had to be set to rise, and the little girl's interest fell away. "Look, Eddie's havin' a snow fight!" Melody, at the kitchen window, jumped up and down in excitement. Hope peeped over her shoulder. Eddie was holding his own in a massive snowball battle. Not much of the drive was being shoveled. But things were happening, in a small way.

The kitchen alarm went off, signalling the beginning of a new schedule which Hope had prodded Ralph into making the night before.

"Your turn," she told the little girl.

"My turn?"

The girl was still jumping up and down, squeezing her thighs together. "Potty time," Hope announced. "Every hour and a half the bell rings and you go off to the potty. Off you go."

"You don't have to come with me?"

"Nope. Big girls learn to do this for themselves. And you're a big girl, right?"

"Right," the child said doubtfully. "Uncle Ralph, he keeps comin' and saying do this and do that and—I gotta run!"

By ten o'clock the two guys had had enough. They tumbled in through the front door, yelling at each other at more decibels than the law allowed, and presented themselves with glowing cheeks and drippy noses at the kitchen door.

"Hot chocolate," Hope announced, "right after you strip yourself out of those winter coats—and wash your face and hands."

"Me too?"

Hope looked at Uncle Ralph, struggling with his heavy boots. "You too," she confirmed. He grinned at her and complied. And that's what I need, she told herself. A little more self-containedness!

Melody came tripping into the kitchen, and sidled up to Hope. "I did it, Aunt Hope. I did it."

"Did what?" Eddie inquired. "Where's the hot bread?"

"The bread's still in the oven," Hope retorted. "It takes time."

"And what did Melody do?"

"Girl's business," Melody announced grandly. The two men glared at her and then raced for the downstairs washstand. Uncle Ralph was back first. He collapsed into his chair with a sigh of relief.

"Been up to something, have you?"

"Who, me?" she asked.

"Don't 'who, me?' me," he said, chuckling. "I've known you for a long time, Little Miss Innocence. What have you been up to with Melody while I've been out training Eddie?"

"Training," she returned smugly. "The way my mother trained me. Any more questions?"

"No, I guess not. You turned out pretty good. If Melody comes out half as well the Jakowski family will owe you a lot."

"A compliment?"

"A real and true compliment."

Compliments from this man were beyond Hope's ken. She blushed and turned away toward the oven.

"Something smells good." His voice was just behind her left ear, whispered instead of spoken. Hope turned around quickly.

"It's only bread," she protested, warding him off with both hands.

"That isn't what I was talking about," he said as he put a hand on each of her shoulders and pulled her soft body up against his. "This is what I mean." His nose was questing somewhere below her earlobe where, some time earlier this morning, she had sprayed a touch of Ma Femme.

She stared up at him, mesmerized. His head came down, gradually filling up her entire range of view, until his lips touched hers. A gentle touch, more like a caress than a kiss.

"Whatcha doin', Uncle Ralph?" Melody was standing in the doorway. "Marrying Miz Hope?"

He broke away and took a deep breath. "Marrying? Who ever thought of such a thing? I'm kissing the cook," he answered. "Just checking to see if she's done yet, you know. Like we have to test the bread."

"Is she done?"

"Oh, Lord, the bread," Hope squeaked. She whirled away from him, snatched up a pot-holder, and opened the oven door. The smell of fresh-baked bread enveloped the kitchen, and just the tiniest bit of smoke. "The bread's done," she announced. *And so am I*, she teased herself. *So am I!*

The snowstorm sputtered to a stop at about six in the evening. Clouds rushed toward the Atlantic Ocean, first in dark masses, and then in shattered splinters, until, about an hour later, a star broke through. But by that time both the children were exhausted, and fast asleep. Downstairs in the warm living room Hope was at work on her knitting, with Rex at her feet.

Ralph lowered his book. "Don't you ever stop?" he asked.

"It's a Christmas present," she returned, holding up the red and white outline of a half-finished child's sweater.

"No need to hurry. Christmas is months away."

"You don't understand. It's for *last* Christmas, for Faith's son Victor. I was so slow that I had to *buy* him something last year."

"And that's a bad thing?"

"It is in the Latimore family. Gifts are supposed to be from heart and hand."

"But buying is easier."

"I suppose so. But that doesn't count. We have fourteen people in our family. We all have trust funds. If we want something we can all buy almost anything for ourselves. Except for Thelma, of course. She's only a baby."

"Yes, of course," he muttered as he picked up his book again, and then put it down. "And you're the only unmarried adult in the family?"

Her fingers stopped and the needles fell into her lap. What in the world is he getting at now? she asked herself. Whenever the men she knew started talking about Latimore money a red flag went up in the back of her mind. She cocked her head and looked at him, sitting across the room by the fireplace. "Yes," she said.

"Nobody wanted to marry you for your money?"

"Lots of people."

"But you didn't fall for any of them?"

"As you see. Of course I had the help of the Latimore Detective Service, under the direction of three company lawyers."

"Wow. Sleeping Beauty!"

"How do you figure that?"

"Your father put you to sleep when you were fifteen, with all those detectives and lawyers to guard you. And now it's time for you to wake up, isn't it?"

"I don't understand you."

"It's time for the royal prince to come along and kiss you awake."

"I don't know what you're talking about. Where do you get all these crazy ideas?"

"Oh, I don't know; they sort of seem to float around in the air, and eventually they land on my nose."

"What a lot of garbage you carry around in your luggage, Ralph Browne."

"You want proof?"

"Impossible."

He carefully inserted a marker in the book he was reading and set it aside. Hope watched with distinct interest. Ralph Browne was about to make a fool of himself, and Hope Latimore was prepared to laugh. He came up out of his chair and walked over to her, crowding into her little couch beside her.

"Comfy?" he inquired as he slipped one arm around her back. Slowly done so as not to startle her. Hope felt a slight feeling of alarm, but in the quiet that followed the feeling passed. "Comfy?" he repeated.

"Well," she drawled, "reasonably so. Now what happens?"

"Stage two." His other arm came around her, crossing just under her breasts, and his hand made a firm anchorage at her lower rib.

"Still comfy?"

"Of course," she said. There was an echo of a nervous little tremor in her voice that they could both hear. She tried to suppress it without much luck.

"And now..."

"And now what?" she asked bravely, the way a half-terrorized girl might.

"And now we fold up the sandwich like this." He proceeded to demonstrate. "And then we kiss the girl gently on her cheek, and on the tip of her nose."

"That tickles."

"And now the piece de resistance." It was what they call in basketball a full-court press. His lips came gently down and sealed her mouth. His two arms tightened and held her helplessly. If she had struggled she might have broken free—but Hope Latimore had no intention of struggling. Instead she sat there beside him with a foolish grin on her face as she assisted in her own seduction.

And there might have been no end to it all, except that Melody Jakowski came thumping down the stairs, towing her old rag doll. "You din't come to read me no story, Aunty Hope," she stated accusingly, as might be expected.

"Tell her to go away," Ralph muttered as he tried to unfold his tangled arms.

"What? Your very own niece?"

"Well, I've got my finger caught in your thingumajig, and I don't seem to be able to get it out."

"You got it in there all by yourself."

"Aunt Hope!" It was a sound of misery. "I brought the book."

"All right, love. Climb up between us and we'll read you a story."

"I can't get my finger out," he growled.

"Pull," Hope coached. He did. There was a ripping sound. Hope groaned. Bras were becoming more and more expensive, even at the Mall. But at least their Siamese-twins act was finished. Melody climbed into her new little nest, sat back with a sigh, and opened her book.

"Ain't it wonnerful," the little girl said, "havin' *two* people to read the stories? Eddie's gonna be mad when I tell him tomorrow."

"Maybe we should keep this our secret," kindly ole Uncle Ralph suggested.

"Oh, I could roust Eddie out of bed in a minute," Hope put in. "He wouldn't mind, and I wouldn't mind—"

"But I would, by damn, mind it," good old Uncle Ralph roared. "Get on with the story before I cloud up and rain all over the pair of you!"

CHAPTER FIVE

MORNING again. Wednesday? Hope groaned and struggled to open at least one eye. She had forgotten to draw the curtains. Bright sunshine almost blinded her. The house was quiet; her bedside clock said midnight, and the hands were not moving. It couldn't be midnight, not with all that bright sunlight, could it?

Hope forced a leg out from under the blankets. The cold floor chilled her bare foot; Rex had stolen her rug again and was huddled half under the bed with the rug in sole possession. She stumbled out of the bed and fumbled for her slippers and robe. The old dog grumbled, rolled over, and went back to sleep again. Hope struggled out into the corridor, flapping her way into her robe.

It was as dark as sin in the corridor, it being illuminated only by the window in her room, behind her. She flipped the light switch. Nothing happened. And there we go, she told herself. A long corridor with all but one bedroom door closed and only two dirty windows, one at each end. She flipped the light switch again. Power failure. Not something new to a country girl. She shrugged and felt her way toward the stairs.

None of the ground-floor lights responded. The kitchen computer was still. But the burners on the gas stove were lit, and the kitchen windows were bright. Ralph Browne sat huddled at the kitchen table, trying his best to read some computer printouts by the window light. A coffee mug was clenched in his hands. He looked up as Hope banged against the kitchen door.

"Ah. Lady Bountiful," he drawled, setting his papers aside.

"Not me," Hope denied. "Lady Sunshine. And that's my sister Faith who works for her—or used to, anyway. And I sure wish I was there."

"You've got me confused. And you wish you were where?"

"In the Caribbean," Hope returned. "St Kitts. They live on the island. I don't believe they've ever had snow there. My sister and her husband." She dropped into the chair across from him and sighed. "Sometimes I wish I— Is that coffee?"

"It is. Sometimes you wish you . . . ?"

"Had some coffee. The children are still asleep?"

He pushed back his chair and fetched her a mug. "Instant," he said as he set it down beside her. "So you've been to the Tropics? A world traveler?"

"Yes and no," she answered as she sipped at the piping hot coffee.

"Yes and no?"

"Yes."

"You are a goldmine of information." There was a sarcastic bite to his words.

"I mean yes, I've been to the Tropics. For my sister's wedding, you know. My brother Michael escorted me. And my mother. I wouldn't have dared to go alone. And no, I'm not a world traveler."

"Hard to believe," he mumbled.

"Try harder."

He groaned. "I've got a whole stack of computer problems to deal with. No electricity, no computer. I'm technologically unemployed."

"There's plenty of snow out there. Must be two or three feet."

"Six feet in the drifts."

"Great fun for the kids."

"By gum, you're right. I'll get Eddie up and out in the snow. He'll have a grand time."

"You also have a niece," she prompted.

"Melody? Girls aren't much good for snow fights. And she's so darn small."

"Try her. You'll find out differently."

"Lady, you are doing your best to upset my way of life, aren't you?"

"Nobody deserves it more." It was said tongue-in-cheek, but nevertheless hardly a week ago she would never have had the nerve to say it out loud at all.

"Thank you very much." He didn't look as if he meant it, either. She sniffed at him and then tasted the coffee. It was terrible. "Damn," she muttered, coughing.

"It *is* bad, isn't it?" He chuckled. "You're the housekeeper. If you had got up earlier we both wouldn't have had to suffer."

Hope pushed back her chair, laid her hands on the coffee pot, and carried it over to the sink. "Blame it all on me," she said dismally as she dumped the lot of it down the sink. "I can't understand how you got along without me."

The laughter in his face faded away. It was a very sober young man who responded glumly, "Me neither." And then, after a pause, he said, "You *are* making more coffee?"

"Not more of the same. Better. Whatever I make couldn't help but be better!" She lit the flame under the kettle and turned around toward him.

"You know what?" he asked.

"No. What?"

"My sister and brother-in-law could be gone a long time. We could all be dead from food poisoning before they get back."

"Food poisoning?" She examined him cautiously. He had that look of idle innocence on his face.

"Food poisoning," he affirmed. "All dead."

"I'd—you have some plan to avoid this terrible fate?"

"I'm in the planning business, Miss Latimore. There's a very simple solution. All you have to do is marry me."

"All I have to do is—*what*?" Hope backed off into the corner of the kitchen. "All I have to...?"

"Marry me. What could be better than that?"

The kettle began to whistle at her. My ear's jammed, she told herself. Marry him? What a joke that would be. Marry the bad Mr Browne?

"You had a good idea last night," he said, interrupting her thoughts.

"Good? I—" Yes, she had, she admitted. Being honest about it. It had been a lot of—fun. But it was not the kind of—fun—that a Latimore girl would seek out. Not on her life. Ma—Mary Kate—would have a fit! "It— it's not the sort of thing a girl can acknowledge," she stuttered. "Besides, I don't think my family would approve of you. Why don't you get the kids and—?"

"Another Latimore method? Never do today what you can put off until tomorrow?"

"Don't push your luck," she spluttered, and she fled the kitchen and took shelter upstairs in her bedroom. She had a shocked expression on her face. Not because of his inane proposal, but rather because she didn't dare to answer.

An hour later little Melody appeared at her half-open door. "Aunty Hope?"

"Yes, dear?"

"Ain't there gonna be no breakfass?"

"Didn't your uncle make you something?"

"He *maked* some oatmeal. I mean some *real* breakfass. Like ham and eggs, an' sausages and bacon and toast and stuff like that."

"Hungry, are you?"

"Starvin'."

Me too, Hope thought as she swung her feet down to the floor. "Me too, love. Come on."

On the way down the stairs they came across a disgruntled little boy. He stopped them with an imperious wave of his hand. "Uncle Ralph said to go upstairs and put on winter warm stuff 'cos we're going out in the snow." Eddie shuddered, as if he could already feel the cold.

"Not me," Melody replied. "Hope and me, we is goin' back down to the kitchen to have some real breakfass. You go ahead." She reached over and took Hope's hand.

"But Uncle said—"

"Uncle Ralph, he's not my favorite uncle no more. Hope is."

"But she can't be your favorite uncle, dummy. She's a girl. Uncles have to be men!"

"Hah! A lot you know!"

"And Uncle Ralph said—"

There was a smirk on the little girl's face as she and Hope clattered down the stairs. And Eddie, despite his uncle's order, followed close behind. Their uncle was still at the table, hunched over his papers, when the trio came in. He looked up at them, the eternal grouch.

"I said to put on your cold-weather gear."

"Don't look at me," the little girl said. "Hope an' me, we're going to have breakfass together. You and Eddie, you can do what you want."

"Breakfast? I made you breakfast."

"No, you din't, Uncle Ralph. You made us lumpy oatmeal. That ain't breakfass."

He stared at them for a moment, and then a big smile washed across his face. "When you're right, you're right," he said as he held out both hands in Melody's direction. She squealed in glee and jumped at him. Her favorite uncle was restored to his former power and position again.

Hope shook her head in disgust. The child was a pushover! Just because Uncle Ralph was solidly masculine, good-looking, with lots of charisma— What in the world am I thinking? she asked herself. She gave herself a good shake and walked over to the gas stove.

"You suppose there'll be enough for three of us?" Eddie asked hopefully. "I really didn't eat much of the oatmeal."

"How about four of us?" their uncle inquired. "I didn't eat much of the oatmeal either."

Hope turned her back on them so that Uncle Ralph couldn't see her grin, and searched out the *big* frying pan.

The snow was cold; the wind was cold; Hope Latimore was cold and wished that she weren't. Uncle Ralph had discovered two Flexible Flyers in the barn. Old, tired sleds, but willing to fly. And the road out to the highway had a sufficient slant to make things go, giving a coasting lane of about a hundred yards before the sled would crash into the piled-up snow left by the plows as they built up a mountain of the white stuff. A clever system, it was. The busy plows, two abreast, cleared the surface of the main road by shutting off access to all the houses along its sides.

"Stupid," Hope murmured as she and Melody made one attempt. Her cheeks were rosy red, her beautiful hair flying in the wind. The most beautiful woman I've seen in years, Ralph Browne told himself as he watched the pair struggling to tow their sled back up the hill.

"Spirit," he cheered from the sidelines. "It takes a lot of spirit to—" But by the time he had the words unwound Eddie had applied a shot of energy to the back end of the male team's sled, and it went zooming down the slide, digging its bow deep into the snowpile at the far end. And of course Uncle Ralph was sitting in front, vainly trying to steer the sled, as it plunged three or four feet into the pile of snow, burying the front end of the sled, and Uncle Ralph as well.

"*Fu-nny*," Eddie chanted, and Melody echoed.

Hope kept her mouth shut. Men had their dignity, she knew, and it in no way matched a child's excitement. So she was actually holding her breath until the snow where the front end of the sled should have been burst upward like a volcanic explosion, and Uncle Ralph came up for air, yelling, "Fu-nny!"

Unfortunately, after five or six runs, the male team came up out of the snow yelling, and proceeded to bombard the female team with loose snowballs. Melody, being the smartest girl in Taunton, ducked behind Hope, who managed to get herself thoroughly soaked, lost her scarf, and her temper as well, and stomped off into the kitchen to restore the blood flow in her nether limbs. Her withdrawal was accompanied by a jeering mob of three, claiming cowardice.

Which was true, Hope admitted to herself as she peeled off a layer or two of sweaters and prepared chocolate-chip cookies—large size—and a pot full of hot chocolate. When she heard the pounding of feet on the front porch she summoned up a big smile, but it wasn't big enough. Eddie came in alone.

"Aunt Hope," he yelled. "Aunt Hope!"

"In the kitchen, love."

"Come quick. Quick. Uncle Ralph, he—"

"He what?" Hope asked as she reached for her heavy outer wear.

"Come 'n' see, Aunt Hope!" And the front door slammed behind him as he ran back out onto the porch.

"So come and see," Hope muttered as she followed him out into the cold, and almost tripped over Rex in the process. Her dog yapped a couple of times at her, and then raced around to the back of the house barking his fool head off, and as she whipped around in the deeper snowdrifts she could hear Melody crying.

It was hard for Hope, short as she was, to run in snowdrifts three feet or more high, but she put her head down and tried. And there they were. Melody at the foot of the hill, crying, Eddie struggling up the snowhill, shouting, about halfway up, and Uncle Ralph, sitting at the top of the hill, using a large number of small words, loudly.

Hope stopped by the baby's side and snatched her up. "You're all right?" she panted.

"Me?" Melody gave her a little hug. "I'm okay. But—"

If it wasn't the little girl it was plain to see that it wasn't the boy. He was still vaulting upward, yelling his heart out, so it must be—Uncle Ralph? Hope set the girl gently down in the snow. "Wait here," she ordered, and started plowing her way upward, using the trail broken by Eddie.

"Wait here," Melody shouted after her. "Always wait here. Don't do that, Mel'dy. Do that, Mel'dy." At which point the child plonked herself down in the snow, thoroughly protected by her acres of sweaters and her red snowsuit, and began a litany of the negatives in her life.

Hope hesitated for a second to look back at the disgruntled but safe child, and then spurred herself onward, catching up with Eddie and then losing ground when she had to break a trail for herself.

"What happened?" she yelled as she passed the boy. He waved his hand upward.

"Uncle Ralph," Eddie yelled. "He wanted to teach us how to she—" And by that time Hope had arrived at the top. She plowed to a stop beside Ralph. He didn't *look* as if anything was wrong, but he wasn't exactly smiling either.

"What—?"

"Don't ask," he muttered.

"You were teaching the children to *she*?"

"That's how they pronounce it in Norway," he said. "Ski. It's pronounced she! In Norway, where I learned to ski!"

Out of breath, Hope dropped to her knees and put a hand on his shoulder. "Do you say so?" she gasped. "You were demonstrating how to—er—*she*, and . . . ?"

"As you can plainly see," he snarled, "I fell down."

"On a little hill like this? You—"

"You laugh lady, and I'll—cut off all your hair."

"Me? Laugh? I wouldn't do a thing like that." But it was hard not to, she admitted to herself. In all the days she had known Ralph Browne he had always been a consummate athlete. "Well, you can't sit out here in the snow all day. Take my arm and I'll help you up." She slipped both her hands under his right arm and prepared to lift. He yelled. She relaxed her grip.

"Now what?"

"You'll find it hard to believe," he said gently. "And I'd prefer to sit here for a while so you could go—"

"You can't do that," she interrupted. "You'll have pneumonia in ten minutes. Come on now, show a little courage. What won't I believe?"

"You won't believe," he said, "that I've broken my damn leg."

Caught off guard, Hope gulped and fumbled for words. "Don't curse," she squeaked. "The children will— What should I do?"

He shook his head. "You are a wonderful creature, Hope Latimore. Now you go back into the house and pick up the telephone and dial 911, and when the emergency operator comes on the line you tell her that you have a stupid male idiot lying on a snowhill at 1638 State Road, and he's broken his stupid left leg just above his stupid left ankle."

"Yes," Hope replied, trying to memorize the instructions. "Stupid idiot—broken his stupid— Yes, I'll be right back. I think." Eddie had just managed to plow his way up beside them.

"Eddie, you stay here with your uncle. He's broken his stupid left leg, and I have to— Stay here!" And off she went, slipping and sliding back down the hill, snatching up Melody on the way to the house. In the living room, where one of the telephones was located, she got a swift reaction from the 911 operator, who listened carefully to her full report and said, "Yes, someone from Morton Hospital will come as soon as possible. We have a lot of that going around today."

"A lot—?" And only at that moment did the baby of the Latimore family realize that she had repeated the message just as Ralph had directed, including a couple of the short four-letter words he had added just as Eddie had come up.

"Yes," the operator said, and added, editing slightly, "Stupid broken legs! Popular activity on these snowy days."

The ambulance and its paramedics—one slim man with half his hair gone and one husky woman with a flowing mass of red hair—arrived not more than twenty minutes after the telephone call. "Broken leg," the team leader announced after a quick study. "He has to go to hospital for X-rays, although it feels like a clean break. Silly thing to do on a snowpile, wasn't it? Insurance?"

"Thank you very much," Ralph said somewhat sarcastically. "My HMO card is in my wallet. Hope, would you bring it to me?" It wasn't really a question. It was a command. The kind that Mary Kate Latimore issued at home.

"You'd better come along with us, Mrs. Browne."

"I—er—there's nobody to watch the children," Hope stammered. Mrs. Browne? It had a nice sound. Not actually something she would like to be, but a nice sound anyway.

Uncle Ralph spoiled it all. "Get the damn wallet," he said gruffly. "And get the kids inside before they catch cold."

He was still grumbling as the paramedics loaded him onto a stretcher and half skidded, half carried him down the snowhill to the waiting ambulance. The woman in the team winked at her. "You can always tell an injured husband," she murmured in passing. "And by the way, they'll probably send him back tonight or tomorrow. I hope his bed's downstairs someplace? He'll probably have to stay in bed for five or six weeks."

There was no need for the siren, but they used it anyway as they felt their way down the driveway, and then took off at speed on the highway.

"Why—?" Eddie began, and was promptly interrupted by his sister.

"Hope, you *tolded* me a big lie!" the girl shouted.

"What?"

"Why did they use the siren?" Eddie demanded. "He wasn't hurt. Well, he told me he wasn't!"

"I think maybe they just liked the excitement." It was the only excuse Hope could think of, and she watched the boy's face and waited for his objection. Instead Eddie just shrugged and stomped off towards the house. Rex followed along with him.

Hope watched the boy's back as he struggled up onto the porch and into the house, and then turned back to the angry little girl's face positioned just in front of her, waiting for her turn.

"You *tolded* me you wasn't gonna marry Uncle Ralph," Melody said sternly. "And you did!"

"I what?"

"You said you wouldn't, and the lady from the ambulance called you Mrs. Browne, and you didn't said you wasn't, and grown-ups ain't supposed to lie to kids! That a terrible thing, lying!"

"Oh, Lord," Hope said, sighing. "It's all a mistake, love. Your uncle and I are *not* married. Not yesterday, not today, not next week! Not! And if I don't figure some way to get him a bed downstairs—"

"Not next week?"

"Not next week!"

"How about next month?"

"No, not next month! How am I going to get a bed downstairs?"

"But if you ain't gonna get married why do you need a bed downstairs?"

Hope took advantage of her years of babysitting experience. With both hands on her hips she glared down at the belligerent little face and said, "Because!" And then stalked off up the stairs. Melody, having no answer to such adult reasoning, followed along behind, her lips going ten miles to the minute as she talked to herself.

Eddie was already in the living room, with a glass of milk and a cookie in hand. "He could sleep here." He gestured toward the fireplace. "He's got a sleeping bag and everything."

"Yes, I'm sure he'd like that." Hope shook her head. Of course Ralph Browne would like that, sleeping on the floor and all. But the living room was well heated, there was a bathroom between it and the kitchen, and— What I need is technical advice, she thought as she reached for the telephone.

"No, we aren't home," a gruff male voice told her.

"Don't you dare hang up on me, Jake Meadows," Hope growled back. She had long since learned to handle her massive brother-in-law. "I need some medical advice."

"Lord love us," Jake said. "You're not ill, baby?"

He was the only one in the world, outside of her mother, that Hope allowed the privilege of "baby"ing her. And now he was yelling for her sister.

"N-no, wait," she stuttered, but she was too late. Her oldest sister, Becky, had snatched the telephone away and, as was usual for an older sister in the Latimore family, began to rearrange the world. "Hope—you're not sick, love?"

"I'm working, and I'm not sick, but the man I— Yes, working. As a housekeeper, and he— No, I said as a housekeeper, and I'm not too proud to work at— Yes, and he broke his leg and the medics took him to Morton Hospital and I— Yes, Mary Kate knows all about it, and— *No!*"

Off stage, so to speak, she could hear Becky half explaining to her doctor husband, "Hope finally found a man. He broke his leg. Morton, I guess..." And then finally she came back on the line. "Don't worry. Jake and I are both on our way. Right now. To the hospital."

"Oh, no," Hope said, groaning. "That's not what I—" But Becky had already hung up.

"You got trouble?" Eddie asked.

"I got a sister," Hope replied glumly.

Eddie, who knew how much trouble sisters could be, just shook his head, and came to stand by Hope's knee as she dialed another number. They waited through four interminable rings before a sweet voice answered, "Latimore Incorporated. May I help you?"

By this time Hope had learned a lesson. As fast as she could go, she said, "My name is Hope Latimore. I have to speak to my brother. It's urgent."

She could almost hear the switchboard operator say something like, "Oh, is that so?" But instead, after a few seconds of cogitation, the operator said only, "Yes, ma'am." Through three separate offices the call advanced. At each station some voice said, "Hope Latimore. Urgent." Until, at the last office called, a very superior secretary heard the alarm, said a very superior, "Yes," and in a flash Michael was on the line. An upset Michael.

"Hope? What is it? Pop? His heart?"

"No. Not Pop. Nobody in the family. It's Uncle Ralph. He broke his leg."

Her brother gave a big, gusty sigh of relief. "I've been worried about Pop," he said, "and I'm sorry that Uncle Ralph broke his leg. It can be very painful. Who the hell is Uncle Ralph? I'm terribly busy, baby!" And that was the next to the last straw. Baby!

"I am *not* the baby in this family. You are!"

"Don't roar at me on the telephone," he said abruptly. "And I'm sorry I said baby. Now, I've apologized twice. I'm sorry that Uncle Ralph broke his leg. But why should Latimore Incorporated worry about that?" And then he embarked on a sideline conversation. He must have put his huge hand over the mouthpiece of the telephone, because she could faintly hear him say to his secretary, "My baby sister's in a tizzy. Tell them I'll be back in a few minutes."

"Tell them you have to come home at once," she snarled at him. "You'll remember Uncle Ralph. He's the computer genius who's saving you millions of dollars by his brain power?"

"You mean Ralph Browne?" There was a little more respect in the voice. "You mean Ralph Browne broke his leg? Dear Lord. Call your sister Becky. Or Jake."

"I don't need Becky *or* Jake," she snapped. "And besides, I've called them already. But neither of them are big enough. I need you and you'd better get moving."

Her brother, she remembered, had attended a charm school to raise his social consciousness. At least that was what he had said. She could hear him as he took ten huge deep breaths and then came back on the line. "Perhaps," he said gently, "you could explain why you don't need the only two doctors in the family because they're not big enough?"

Hope was getting desperate by this time. Desperate and angry. "Because of the bed," she said slowly. "Anybody could see that."

"Of course. Because of the bed."

"You don't understand," Hope said, sighing. "Nobody understands!" And much to her disgust a tear slipped down her cheek. "I don't deserve this. I really don't."

Latimore women never cried. Not even the baby of the family, Michael told himself. "Hope," he said gently, "imagine that I'm only sixteen, got it?" She nodded.

Eddie prodded her. "He can't hear you when you shake your head," the boy coaxed.

"Yes, I've got it."

"Now, tell me in real short sentences."

"Yes," she said, and cleared her throat. "Ralph Browne slipped on a snowslide this afternoon. He fell down. He broke his leg. The ambulance came. They said he would be back home very soon. They said he would have to sleep on the ground floor." Eddie shook her arm again.

"Not sleep on the floor," he coached. "Sleep on a bed on the ground floor."

"Yes," Hope said, and made the correction. "Only we don't have a bed on the ground floor. And all his computer stuff is on the attic floor. And he has to probably spend five or six weeks in bed, the medic said."

"Whoa up," her brother said. "And that's why you need a big man—maybe even two or three big men—to move all that stuff down to the ground floor?"

"Thank God," Hope Latimore said as she knuckled the tears out of the way. "And if you don't he won't be able to do your work and I won't be able to—"

"Calm down, love," he said. "And *you* won't be able to—what?"

Eddie Jakowski was only eight, but he hadn't come down in the last snowstorm. He pulled the telephone handset out of Hope's hand and completed the sentence. "Kiss him," he said. Hope snatched the telephone back.

"He's a nice kid," she said, "but he's only eight. What would *he* know?"

"Quite a bit," her brother said. "I can remember that far back myself, but then of course you've never been a boy, have you?"

"I don't understand, Michael Latimore, how you can run that great big company. I really don't understand. I could do without all this trouble."

"Well, I don't know," he said gently. "Maybe you ought to talk it over with Mary Kate. All I know is that after all this you're the one who's crying. Doesn't that tell you something?"

If he were only closer, Hope thought, I'd hit him. "No, it doesn't tell me a thing," she muttered—after she had hung up the telephone.

CHAPTER SIX

JAKE MEADOWS was the first to arrive, slipping and sliding up the drive in his big Cadillac. Barely six feet tall, and weighing a lot more than he had when Hope had first met him, he appeared to be a grizzly bear, with a salt-and-pepper beard and the best surgeon's hands in New England. He climbed slowly out of the car, and stomped snow as he plowed his way up onto the porch. An impressive man. Hope, waiting at the top of the stairs, could remember she had called him Mr. Meadows until five years after he had married her oldest sister, Becky. And now she threw herself down the stairs at him, and he caught her casually as a big man could.

"Jake, I'm so glad you came."

"Didn't need a surgeon," he assured her. "Becky's looking after him, so I thought I'd come along and see how our little pint of peanuts was making out." And as casually as he had caught her flying body he carried her into the house. Melody stood at the door of the living room, and was properly introduced. When he set Hope down the little girl walked around him carefully.

"Big," she pronounced. "Boyfriend?"

"My sister married him," Hope explained glumly.

"Ah. You was too slow?"

"I was just a little older than you are when I met him."

"That's good."

"What, may I ask, is this all about?" Jake asked.

"She wants to get me married off," Hope explained. "What about Ralph?"

"Nothing really bad," he said as he struggled out of his coat. "They'll plaster him up and have him home tonight. In fact, Becky has her station wagon; she'll probably drive him back. Now just who and what is this young man, that he stirs up the whole Latimore tribe?"

"I thought you was a bear," Melody put in. "Until you took your coat off. You ain't, are you?"

"No, indeed, young lady. I'm a surgeon. Hope, I'm afraid your sister is going to be mad at you for crying wolf. Now kindly answer my question."

Hope shrugged. She knew full well that Jake Meadows would not shut down until he had the answer he wanted. "Housekeeper," she murmured. "I'm his housekeeper. Just his housekeeper."

"Now that's a laugh," her brother-in-law said. "Just like your sister was housekeeper to Lady Sunny?" Hope had the grace to blush. "So all right, why did you call us, a surgeon and a cardiologist?"

"Well, all I wanted was some information about how you treat a man with a broken leg when you get him home, and before I could ask you started passing the telephone around and—"

"Infuriating, isn't it?" He chuckled and sat down on the sofa. "Doctors think they know everything."

"That isn't what bugs me," she returned. "It's just— you all treat me as if I were some little kid. I'm not, you know."

"Yes, I know, but I forget," he acknowledged.

"What's a surgeon?" Melody insisted on knowing. Jake moved to a chair and sat down, just as Eddie came in from the kitchen.

"Nice pizza, Hope. A surgeon is a big fish in the ocean."

"That's a sturgeon," Hope corrected. "Dr. Meadows is a surgeon."

"I knowed he wasn't no fish." Melody stuck her tongue out at her brother and dodged behind a chair, just in case. "Men! They all think they know everything."

They really do, Hope mused. She's only three, and I didn't find that out until I was fifteen!

There might have been something more to say, but at that moment feet thundered up the front steps and the door burst open.

"Now where the devil is that bed?" her brother demanded as he strode in. Her father was right behind him.

"My goodness," Melody muttered as she ducked behind Hope's skirts. "He's bigger."

"That's my dad."

"And him, that other one, he's the biggestest in the world."

"That's my brother, love. And you may be right."

And behind them, shadowed by the lamps, was another big man. When he stepped forward into the light Hope drew a quick breath and tried to back away. Alfred Pleasanton! "Oh, Michael, what have you done to me?" she muttered under her breath. She tried her best to shrivel away into invisibility, with no success.

"We'd better get on with it," her father said. "Your mother went over to the hospital, and if we don't have this all fixed up by the time she gets here—well, your ma is a little bit bossy, you know."

"Just a little bit," Hope murmured. "Lucky I didn't inherit any of that."

Hope Latimore didn't understand why, but all of them turned and gave her a suspicious stare. There was a brief pause, and then conversation broke out again.

"Let's clear all this furniture away, and then we can move the other stuff in," her father said as he looked around. Eddie decided to stay to help.

With the three husky men at work Hope managed to resist being the Indian Chief. Mary Kate would be along soon enough to fill that job. Instead she bustled Melody into the kitchen, closed the door, and began to work on more pizza.

"Eddie got to stay," the little girl complained. "Just because he's a boy, I 'spect?"

"No, love," Hope told her, "because he's eight years old. Besides, you wouldn't want to get caught in that crowd. Remember how big they all are? They might step on you, and what a squash that would be. And remember how much pushing and carrying there is to be done? That's what men are for."

"Pushin' and carryin'?"

"Exactly. And you mustn't forget that. Women are made of sugar and spice and everything nice. Men are made of—"

"Puppy dogs' tails," Melody interrupted. "My mummy told me that, a long time ago. Men ain't very nice."

"Oh, that's where you're wrong," Hope told her. "Men are very nice to have around."

"For pushin' an' carryin'!"

"And one or two other things."

"Like kissin'?"

Hope took a deep breath. "Have a slice of pizza," she suggested. Her face was blush-red again. From the oven heat, she assured herself. *Would I lie to a kid?*

Within the next fifteen minutes another car drove up into the driveway, and there was an increase in the speed of labor next door. Mary Kate had arrived. She had a few words to say to the laborers next door, and then

walked into the kitchen and plumped herself down in
Uncle Ralph's favorite chair. In the other room there
was a significant increase in speed among the working
people. "Men need to be organized," she announced.
"Is that pizza I smell?"

"Yes, ma'am."

"Proper place for the women to be," the doyenne of
the Latimore family commented. She dropped her heavy
purse under the table, drew up a second chair and rested
her tiny feet on it. "Now, somebody tell me how this
silly business happened."

"Would you like a cup of coffee?" her daughter offered hesitantly.

"First I'll have a mug of coffee, yes, and *then* I'll
have the information." There was a slight touch of the
whiplash, but only a slight touch. Melody stepped into
the gap out of ignorance.

"Uncle Ralph was on top of the snow mountain and
he said something like, 'Watch how you do a—'"

"Cartwheel on skis," Eddie interrupted as he walked
in.

"Yeah, one of them." She paused. "He's my brother,
Eddie. He knows lotsa things. For a boy, that is."

"Wipe your nose, Melody."

"Yeah. I did. So then he *she'd* up to the top of the
mountain an' got up some speed and then he jumped
up and did a tumblesault, only he didn't land on his
skis, and there was this cracking noise and there he was
sittin' on his bum. 'An' what do you know?' he said,
and then he said, 'Oh—' and one of those words that
sounds like 'it' that Eddie and I aren't supposed to use,
but it begins with a 's'."

"Melody!"

"Well, he did, Aunt Hope. An' then he yelled real loud for Hope. But not us, just Hope. He yells a lot for Hope, 'specially when he's in trouble.

"And then Eddie says, 'You done that too fast. You gotta show us again' and Uncle Ralph said somethin' like, 'Get help, kid.'"

The little girl wiped her nose again. "And then Hope comed runnin' out, and everything was OK again and that's what happened."

"And very nicely told," Mary Kate said. "Very nice. And my daughter got everything straightened out? How nice."

"Hope always gets everything straightened out," Eddie chimed in. "She's our housekeeper, you know. That's a very hard job."

"And if my ears don't deceive me here comes my other daughter with her station wagon and the patient."

"Oh, my," Hope said. "You kids stay out of the way now." And she rushed through the house to the front door. As announced, it was her sister Becky and her battered blue station wagon. The back seat of the station wagon was folded down, and flat on the floor, on a canvas stretcher, was Uncle Ralph. At the same moment the working party stomped down the stairs with his bed.

"Nothing serious," Becky reported.

"Huh! A lot *you* know," Ralph grumbled from his bed of pain.

"Oh, shut up," Hope snapped. "She's the second-best doctor in the Commonwealth, and if you hadn't been so busy showing off all this would never have happened."

"Second best?" Becky queried.

"That's what I need," Ralph groaned. "A cheerful little welcome."

"W-well . . ." Hope stuttered.

"Get me out of here," Ralph commanded.

"Take your time," Becky told him. "It's only a broken leg, not a major catastrophe. Besides, you can't expect a doctor to carry patients around. Now, Hope, about this—second best?"

"I have to get some help. Carrying help," Hope muttered as she turned back to the door and stuck her head in. "Hurry up," she yelled. "He's here." Several groans greeted her.

"I just this minute sat down," her father said.

"And he's getting old," her brother Michael reminded her.

Nobody stirred.

"Ma's in the kitchen," Hope said firmly. Everybody stirred.

An hour later the confusion had settled, and the various Latimores had fled the scene, leaving only the family and Alfred Pleasanton. Uncle Ralph was dozing on the bed in the former living room. Both children had been bathed and put to bed.

"And what brought you to us tonight?" Hope perched herself nervously on the wooden chair.

"Well . . ." Pleasanton laughed. "I've been re-hired at Latimore Inc, and your brother needed help. So naturally I—volunteered."

"I'm sure you did," she returned softly. "And now?"

"I've nothing to go home to," he said. "So I thought that you and I could have a talk about things."

"Things?"

"Hey, you're a lovely little lady." He was a big man with a big voice. It boomed around the ground floor of the house. Hope winced as he came up out of his chair and towered over her.

"I don't see what *things* we could talk about," she said firmly. "I told you some time ago that I—"

She stood up quickly, hardly matching him in size. His big hands fell on both her shoulders.

"You're *my* girl," he said, and gave a little squeeze. Hope gasped at the pain.

"Turn me loose," she demanded, and pushed against his unyielding stomach.

"It was only a little misunderstanding," he insisted. "Forget about it, and let's go back to our original plans." He leaned toward her, as if he meant to kiss her.

"Don't you dare," she yelled. Surprised, he loosened his grip. She dodged away from him.

"Don't make a big thing out of it," he said as he stalked her.

The rearrangement of furniture had blocked all but one door—the one that led to the kitchen. "As I remember, your original plan was just sex," she told him. "And that's not on." He was between her and the door.

"Hope, you know that's not true."

"Hah!"

"We were going to be married. Naturally I expected a little preliminary sexual fun."

"Fun? You think attempted rape is fun?"

"Sex is fun," he said. "All we need is mutual consent."

"And I don't." Her mind was running at full speed. There seemed to be no way out of the problem, and there was hardly any way she could fight him off. What to do?

"Come on now, girl, you'll love it."

And there was an answer! "I probably will, with my husband," she said firmly.

"Now. I'm the man," he boasted. "And now's a good time for a sample, right?"

"Wrong," she said. "I'm engaged to Ralph." She gestured toward the bed without looking. After all, Uncle Ralph was out of action. So what he might hear...

"You're kidding," Alfred said. "That little shrimp?"

"He's three times the man you are. And we're already engaged."

A shutter seemed to drop down over Alfred's eyes, as if he had donned an iron mask to shut out any sort of pleasantness. "Well, I don't believe it," he said. "And I believe I'll have a sample tonight."

"You'd better believe it." The voice came from the bed behind them. Both of them whirled around. Uncle Ralph was up on his elbows, a smile on his face. "I didn't think you wanted to announce it immediately, Hope. But now that you have we might as well go madly ahead. Who is this long drink of water?"

"A-Alfred," Hope stammered. "Alfred Pleasanton. He—"

"Yes, I know what he—" Ralph broke off. "Come over here, sweetheart." He patted the side of his bed. She sidled around Pleasanton and squirmed up to Ralph's side.

Pleasanton seemed to swell up, like an over-inflated balloon. "Surely you don't think you can prevent me from doing whatever I want?"

"Uncle Ralph?" Eddie was standing in the doorway, carrying something. Hope ducked her head. There was bound to be a small riot, and she didn't want Eddie involved. Her eye caught the corner of the fireplace, where a heavy poker stood in its little stand. If I can just slide by Alfred and snatch it up...she thought.

"Is this what you wanted, Uncle Ralph?" Eddie asked.

"The very thing," Ralph said.

Hope couldn't see what they were talking about. Her eyes were moving from the poker to Pleasanton—who suddenly turned very red-faced and backed off across the room.

"Hey, it was only a joke," the big man said weakly. He lifted both hands in front of him as if hoping to defend himself from imminent catastrophe.

"Yeah, funny," Ralph said. "I'd laugh but my foot hurts."

Hope, who was still watching Pleasanton, with her mouth half-open, turned gently around to see behind her. Eddie was standing at the head of the bed, a large grin on his face. Uncle Ralph had fallen back on the pillows, a grin on *his* face, and what appeared to be a revolver in his hand.

"I—where—?"

"I had to go to the bathroom, and I heard him," the boy said.

"Yes, is it—?"

"Loaded? Yes, it is." Ralph flicked back the hammer. It clicked very satisfactorily but Hope, being a sceptic, made a dash for the fireplace and snatched up the heavy poker.

"I'd suggest you better go home," she said. "We thank you for your help in moving the furniture—"

"And suggest you never come back again," Ralph interrupted.

"Yes, I—don't remember where I left my coat."

"Then I guess you'll have to go home without it," Hope said. It was more a command than a suggestion. She wiggled the poker like a baseball bat.

"The door's out here," Eddie said, and made a half-bow as Rex wandered into the room. The dog, who liked everyone in the world except the postman—and Alfred Pleasanton—waddled across the room to Alfred's side, growled a couple of times, and lifted up his right rear leg in a suggestive manner.

"Oh, Lord," Pleasanton muttered as he made a dash for the front door.

"Thirty-six seconds," Ralph said as he consulted the clock on his bedside table. "From bedside to running motor. Not bad for a big guy. You can put the poker down now, love."

Hope hugged the poker to her shaking breast and tried to calm down. "I'm afraid of guns," she said with a gasp. "Is it loaded?"

Ralph laughed. "Not exactly." He seemed amused and Hope was sure she saw a look pass between him and Eddie. Sharing some private joke, no doubt at Hope's expense. "Who would keep a loaded gun in a house where children live? Go to bed, Eddie."

"But Uncle Ralph, it *is* . . ."

"Go to bed, Eddie. You did good tonight, lad."

"But it's. . ." Eddie began, then caught his uncle's look and grinned at them both. "I'm proud of me too," he finished before dashing for the stairs.

Hope edged closer to the bed, cautiously, curiously. Close enough to realize that the gun in question seemed to be made of rather more plastic than guns should surely be. Though Hope had to confess that her experience more or less entirely consisted of late-night cop shows on television.

"You're sure it's not loaded?" she asked suspiciously.

"Well," said Ralph, smiling, "let's see." On the far side of the room was a large mirror with a shelf below it. He aimed the gun in that direction. "See that silver cup?"

Hope turned to look, heard a little click, and the gun went off. She expected a crack of thunder, maybe smoke, certainly plenty of noise. Instead, peering through her fingers, she saw a steady jet of water spurting from the barrel, hitting the cup with accuracy if not much else.

The cup teetered on the edge of the mantelpiece for what seemed an age and then banged into the fireplace.

Ralph roared with laughter. "Eddie obviously never got round to showing you what he got for Christmas..." he managed as his chuckles subsided.

Reality dawned slowly. "A water pistol?" Hope offered at last. "But you let me think... And Alfred... How could you? I ought to hit you with this poker!" she snapped at him as she slowly made her way back to her feet. "Imagine having to live with such a—"

"Just don't hit my leg," he interrupted. "My favorite award, that cup. It might rust."

"I'll favorite you," she muttered as she braced herself against the bed.

"Don't talk to me like that," he said gently. "You'll remember that we're engaged to be married?"

"We're what?"

"Engaged to be married. You remember. You told Alfred that—"

"Th-that was only a—subterfuge," she stuttered at him, so angry that her eyes were sparking. "A distraction!"

"Well, you distracted him."

Hope, who was still clutching the poker to her breast, threatened him with it. "I'll distract—"

"Did he come back? Did you kill him?" It was little Eddie, peering around the corner of the door, Rex behind him, and Melody behind the shaggy old dog, clinging to his collar for support.

"No, Lord, no," Uncle Ralph said, chuckling. "He's gone. That was just a celebration you heard. What are you two doing up so late at night?"

"Tryin' to find out what you two are doing up so late at night," Melody said.

Uncle Ralph was fumbling for an excuse, and Hope was not about to help him. He looked at her, appealing. She sniffed at him and walked over to the fireplace to replace the poker. It was obviously a mistake. She had reminded him of something.

"We were celebrating," he said smoothly. "Your aunt and I have decided to get married. What do you think of that?"

"Oh, wow!" Eddie ran across the room to Hope and hugged as high as he could reach. Melody, without a word, dived for her uncle, missed the huge cast that surrounded his leg, and began to cry all over him. He cradled her head against his chest for a moment.

"What's the matter, little bit? I thought you'd like that. And when your mother and father get back you'll have another house where you can spend a vacation. Why the tears?"

"B'cause," the little girl said as she sat up and tried to dry her eyes on his bedsheet. "B'cause you'll get married and then you'll order some babies and you won't care about me at all!" She sniffed away the tears. "An' then you won't be my nice nuncle!"

"Hey," Uncle Ralph said as he pulled her back down to his shoulder. "No matter what happens I'll always be your Uncle Ralph. See, Eddie understands, don't you, lad?"

The boy moved a little closer to Hope. "Of course," he said. "But when you get married, Aunty Hope, could you teach my mother to make fine breakfasts the way you do?"

Hope ran her hand through his brush of hair. Not cute, like his sister, but a good heart, she told herself. It would be nice to have a boy around the house—as well as a girl?

"And now," Uncle Ralph said, "I need a little rest. Hope, why don't you take this pair back to bed? And then you can come back and settle me down."

And so Hope Latimore, her mind still wandering around all the things Ralph had *not* said, her heart still debating what he *had* said, took both the children in hand and ushered them back to their beds. After which she stopped in the upstairs bathroom to pretty herself and then hurried back downstairs to argue this totally insane business about Hope Latimore and Ralph Browne getting married—a most ridiculous idea, if ever she had heard one. But by that time Uncle Ralph was fast asleep, and snoring.

She gently rearranged his pillows and the snoring stopped. She had learned that much from her mother. But she had not learned how to go to sleep herself, sitting in a narrow wooden chair. So she paced the ground floor of the house for a few minutes, snatched up a couple of the leftover pizza slices, and gnawed at them as she paced.

Getting married? I'm only twenty-four years old, she reminded herself. All of my sisters were much older than that. Maybe there's a law against marrying before you're twenty-four? There were so many laws in the Commonwealth!

She wandered back into the sickroom and watched him sleep, by firelight. He's a great deal like Eddie, she mused. In fact, he's sort of handsome! And the children? Of course they're not *his* children. He's just borrowed them for a time. How would he be without the children? How would he be with children of his own? Children of *our* own? The idea excited her.

There were a couple of spare pillows at the foot of his bed. She stole them both, made a little burrow for herself on the thick living-room rug, and fell asleep. And didn't wake until Rex, trying to slurp up the cold pizza in her hand and missing, landed his wet tongue on her nose. It was morning.

CHAPTER SEVEN

As THE months rolled on toward spring, Ralph Browne gradually descended from a cheerful patient to a grumpy employer, and the healthier he got, the worse he acted. The snow melted away to dirty slush, and then ran off into the gutters and disappeared. So by the time Ralph was free to wander the house on crutches and a walking cast Hope Latimore had come to the conclusion that she should have murdered him while she had the chance.

She said that just a little too loudly when she was beating up bread dough in the kitchen one fine day, and little ears heard her.

"You gonna killed Uncle Ralph?"

"I *should* have."

"I like Uncle Ralph."

"Me too, batter-dipped and deep fried, with a spicy salsa sauce."

At just at that moment Hope's intended menu clomped down the hall and into the kitchen behind them for the ten thousandth time in one morning. "Hope, whatever happened to my football award mug?"

"You shot it."

"That was the most important award I ever won!"

"Don't look at me. You're the one that shot it. Right in the belly button and bounced it into the fireplace."

"But I looked in the fireplace."

"You better watch out," Melody shrilled at him. "She's gonna killed you. Dead, she said."

"No, you don't understand, child," he said. "She's not going to kill me, she's going to marry me."

113

"Maybe there's no difference between the two," Hope grumbled.

"Dead, she said," the little girl chanted as she danced around the pair of them. "Dead, she said. Dead, she said."

"Melody, stop that!" It was a military command, such as any mother would give.

"But you said that," the child reminded her.

"But I didn't mean it," Hope said. "I was angry. People who are angry say strange things. Now you go up to your room and do your homework."

Melody glared at her, and stalked off. Hope, who had learned a lot about kids in the past three or so months, pretended not to notice when the child stuck her tongue out as she went through the kitchen doorway.

"Homework? She might get homework, but not until she gets into school," Ralph said, chuckling.

"You know the major difference between you and me?" she snapped. "You never were a little girl."

"Yes, that's ever so true. And?"

"And I was. I've convinced Melody that she has to do homework. She's been doing lessons every day for an hour—just looking at picture books and drawing, mostly, but it keeps her quiet."

"Lord, what a devious person you are."

"Not me. My mother. She pulled the same scam on me when I was three years old. I don't forget many things like that."

"But you didn't get mad?"

"I've worshipped that lady since for ever. When I find a good thing I stick with it. Watch what you're doing. You're the worst walker on crutches that I've ever seen."

"So you're not prepared to kill me? I'm glad you didn't mean that," Ralph said as he moved closer, balancing not too skillfully on his crutches.

"A lot *you* know," Hope snapped.

"You *did* mean it?"

"Every blessed little bit of it. Ralph Browne, you are getting to be the biggest pain in the—er—neck I've ever known. Well, maybe the second biggest. There's always Alfred Pleasanton to be considered."

"Oh, having met the guy, I can understand why you've put him on your death list." Ralph looked at her curiously. "There's more, isn't there? What happened?"

"He wanted us to get married. Well, that's what he told my mother."

"And what did he tell you?"

"He wanted to—well, you know what he wanted and I wouldn't. I don't give samples. So he tried to take me. I don't want to talk about that any more."

"And he tried to take you?"

"It's called attempted rape. I don't want to talk about that!"

"But your brother brought him along to help with the labor?"

"I didn't tell Michael about the attempted rape. I was afraid— Michael has a bad temper, as do I. But Michael—he's so big that Lord knows what he would have done. I wouldn't want my only brother arrested for murder and mayhem."

"I'm lucky you love me," he said softly.

"You—what?"

"Don't scream, love. It's not polite."

"I love you? You really have a loose screw! I love your niece and your nephew, but you—!"

"Maybe I could take lessons from the kids?" He shifted his weight on the crutches and then—it appeared—the pad on his unbroken leg slipped. He wavered back and forth a time or two.

"Good Lord." Hope stretched out both hands, and when he fell he landed with his arms across both her shoulders. His crutches clattered to the floor.

Flustered, Hope held tight. "Hang on," she said, not knowing what else to say.

"Yes," he said. His mouth was at her ear. She could feel and hear his hot, sweet breath, and the pounding of his heart, faster than she had ever known hearts to beat before. His left arm slipped off her shoulder and fastened itself around her waist. "Don't worry, I'll get it right in a minute," he muttered.

What am I doing? she asked herself. He was pressing close against her, from shoulder to thigh, and she was standing there like a brood mare, waiting. Waiting for what? she asked herself. *What is he doing?* It was a sort of rhetorical question. She knew exactly what he was doing, but neither wanted to admit it nor wanted him to stop. She hugged him tighter.

He seemed to slip down her body. In any event, his face came down to match hers, and his lips closed on hers. Unprepared she definitely was. But it was nice; definitely nice. Warm and wet and—spicy?

And before she could turn it into some long-term osculatory delight the front door slammed.

"I'm home," Eddie yelled as he threw his book bag down the corridor like a bowling ball. "What are you two doing?"

"It's a game," his uncle Ralph snarled. "Don't you have something extra to do at school?"

"Not me," the boy said, chuckling. "I know what you're doing. Smooching! I need a snack, Aunt Hope."

"Youth must be served," Ralph muttered as he pushed himself up and away. "Dammit!"

"Your uncle slipped on his crutches and I had to catch him," Hope tried to explain. "Move that chair behind him so I can set him down."

"Oh, sure." It was the most unbelieving statement one could have heard, but he did move the chair, and helped his uncle down. "There. Now, about my snack..."

Hope flexed her shoulder muscles to relieve the strain. "Peanut butter and jelly?"

"We don't got no pizza?"

"Don't have any," his uncle corrected.

"I can't make pizza every day, Eddie. With your uncle—er—crippled—"

"I am *not* crippled!" he interrupted.

"Yes. I mean, no, of course you're not; you're—"

"Incapacitated."

"Yes. Like you said."

They both stared at her.

"You might as well make some pizza," Ralph coaxed. "I could use a piece or two myself. And you've got a whole pile of dough sitting there on the table."

"Pizza today, no homemade bread tomorrow."

Neither of them was impressed by the edict. "A bird in the hand...?" Ralph suggested.

Hope threw up her hands hopelessly. "I'm never going to get married," she said glumly. The two of them stared at her.

"Or if I do I'm never going to have children. Not a one."

The stares continued. "Well, not more than two," she said, going down to defeat. "Pizza."

Luckily she had the dough ready. With considerable skill, and three cans of sauce, the pizza was ready to come out of the oven in thirty minutes.

"Look at that!" Eddie exclaimed. "Magnificent! I wish my mother could bake like that. I really do."

Hope set the pizza tray down on the table. "You mustn't talk like that," she chided. "Your mother's been sick for such a long time. When she's better—when they get back—you'll see how much better she does everything—when she gets back."

"I know. Cut the pizza," Eddie said. "We'll eat it all before Melody comes down from—"

There was a clatter on the stairs. "Whatcha makin'?" Melody, posing in the kitchen doorway, sniffed, with a suspicious look on her face. "Pizza! And you wasn't gonna save none for me, was you, Eddie Jakowski!"

"Of course I was," the boy said, but his face turned blush-red, giving him away.

"What a bad brother you is, Eddie. Aunty Hope, y'oughta send him straight to his room an' make him close the door!"

"If we do the pizza will be cold," Ralph told her. "Let's eat it first." And, with that magnificent feat of logic, they did.

The children went to bed quietly that night. Hope had long since fallen into a regime of baths and stories and cuddling, and then, tired, wandering downstairs, and this evening was no exception.

Ralph was sitting on the edge of his bed, all of his supper consumed. He turned and smiled at her as she came in to check on him.

"I've been a real pain in the you-know-what," he said.

"I don't remember anybody else in the world who was worse," she agreed, sighing. "Are we going to do better?"

"I shouldn't be surprised. I can see that if I'm going to get you to the altar I've got to change my ways. Right?"

"Right. I mean, not a chance. Even if you improve one hundred percent I don't think I'd want to marry—especially you."

"Of course." He patted the bed beside him, and for some foolish reason that she didn't understand Hope went to him. He put one arm around her shoulders. "Tired?"

She allowed her head to drop onto his shoulder. "Would you believe my mother raised five children, and I never, ever heard her complain about a thing? Of course my sister Becky was almost grown-up when they got married, and my sister Mattie was pretty old too, and they helped. I guess I don't have the stamina for the work."

"Don't kid yourself," he murmured. "Your mother had your father to help, didn't she?"

"Yes, of course."

"And they loved each other?"

"Of course they did. I mean, they still do."

"So, when you fall in love you'll find things will go easier. Love paves a lot of roads, you know."

"I didn't know that." She relaxed against him and tucked her feet up underneath her. His arm tightened across her shoulders. "You know a lot about things like that for a guy who's never been in love."

"Me? I've been in love a dozen times or more, starting way back to when I was in high school."

"Oh, come on, now. Remember I knew you when you were in high school." But curiosity overcame her. "How in the world could you tell you were in love?"

"Lots of ways. First of all, whenever I found myself comfortable with my arm around a girl, and was able to relax, that was one sign."

"That's just sex," she said stiffly. But he has his arm around me now, and I feel—comfortable! she thought.

Is that what it is—just sex? How did I feel, way back in those high-school days? He put his arm around me more than once in those days. Love? If we hadn't been so disrupted at that dance and all, would we have fallen in love? Romeo and Juliet, they were barely teenagers when they— Was that love?

"Don't forget," he added, "that sex is a part of loving. A big part."

"Now you're beginning to sound like Alfred Pleasanton. What else?"

"I could have gone all night without you mentioning that creep. Anyway, how about sharing? My dad told me once that if you look at a girl and feel that you might even be willing to share a toothbrush with her that's love."

"Ugh!"

"That's just a sample. How about this? If you kiss, and it's warm and gentle and tasty, that's a sign of love."

Is it really? she thought. He kissed me, and that's just what it felt like!

"Let me show you." He tugged at her shoulder. She turned and found herself lying across his knees. Then he lifted her up so that her mouth was close to his. And touched her with those warm, sweet lips.

What is it that's going on? she asked herself as she seemed to go into a trance. Warm, moist, tasty? A little shiver ran up and down her spine. He didn't taste like flowers in May. He tasted like—pizza! Warm, sweet, moist, and with both mushrooms and Portuguese linguíça sausage and cheese and—

"See?" He had broken the contact at her lips, but both his arms were around her, squeezing slightly. He dropped a little touch of a kiss on her forehead. It was sweet and comforting, but no pizza. And another shiver ran up and down her spine.

That's what it is, she told herself. Soft, warm, moist—
and pizza. No wonder Italian girls seem to have all the
fun!

"No response?" he coaxed.

"I'm thinking, I'm thinking."

"Maybe I should add just a little touch more sex?"

"I—"

But he cut her off, lifting her up again and sealing off
her lips, putting her words to flight. Warm, moist,
pleasant—and then his hand shifted and came down
gently on her breast. Alarm bells went off in Hope
Latimore's head. They kept ringing—or was it her ears
that were ringing? she wondered.

I ought to stop him, her New England upbringing told
her. I ought to get off his knees and slap his face. I ought
to— What do you suppose he'll do next?

And the answer almost made her break out in tears.

He gently released her lips, sighed, swung her up and
slid her off his lap. She sat on the bed, drooping like a
marionette whose strings had been cut.

"Now then," he said. "What do you think of that?"

She squirmed away from him. Just enough so that
their thighs were not touching. She coughed a time or
two.

"Hmm?"

"I—it was—interesting." Barely in control of herself,
she slid off the bed, adjusted her crumpled skirt, worked
up a small-size smile, and turned around to glare at him.

"You wouldn't care to try another sample?"

"Not—not just this minute," she spluttered. "I think
I need to go up to bed and you need to—"

"Yes, I understand. A guy can't win them all. Maybe
we could try again tomorrow?"

"Maybe." She leaned over and kissed his forehead,
then ran for the stairs before he could lay a hand on her.

"Coward," he yelled after her. She was willing to admit the charge, but didn't plan to stop and debate it.

Rex, who was half-asleep on her rug, opened one eye and watched as she pirouetted back and forth from window to door to window, wanting to sing, but knowing it would waken the kids, and then she would be up half the night trying to explain. And she didn't *have* an explanation.

Sharply at six the next morning she woke up. That handbell next to his bed kept ringing, almost as loudly as the town fire alarm. Groggily she rolled out of her warm bed, managed to find her slippers, and ran for the stairs. Neither of the children stirred. She was out of breath as she swung around his door. He was sitting up on the edge of the bed, just the way he had been the night before.

"What is it?"

"I can't find it." He fumbled around among his blankets.

"You can't find what?"

"I can't find my modem."

"Your what?"

"My modem. The gadget I use on my computer output so I can send messages on the telephone line."

She shook her head in disgust. "Look, buster, it's six o'clock in the morning. The children are asleep and I ought to be! Why do you need to send a message?"

"Because, lady, I plan to get married. And to get married I need to make a lot more money than I've got."

"I would've thought it was more important to track down a woman who's willing to marry you." She walked across the room and collapsed in one of the chairs. "And this time of day is no time to be woman-hunting."

"Oh, I don't know about that. Besides, I've already found her."

His statement startled her. Just the morning after her rejection, and he had already found a replacement! For a second or two her lower lip trembled. But *I* don't care, she told herself fiercely. I don't! He could find a thousand women and—

"Hand me the telephone," he commanded. "Where the devil is that modem?"

Hope slipped down lower in her chair and sneered, to emphasize her lack of interest. And there it was. "You're sitting on it," she said casually.

"The telephone?"

"The modem." She got up and brought the telephone over to his bedside. He fumbled around under his pajamas and retrieved the modem.

"Now, what the devil is that telephone number of your brother's operations office?"

She knew it by heart. As she did the three other main numbers in the executive office. A girl had to know where her bread and butter came from. She spat it out at him and watched while he dialed the number. And the extra two digits which connected him to the Latimore fax room.

"You're calling my brother?"

"Not exactly. He won't be up yet."

"Ha! You don't know my brother. Or my father either. One of them will have been there since five in the morning. My mother hates that."

He reached over and connected a couple of plugs, and then touched the transfer key on his computer. The machine chuckled at him for a minute or two, and then turned itself off.

"What—?"

"Your sister Mattie is still in the Sudan with her railroad and she called me last night with a problem. That was the answer."

"You've been up all night?"

"Why not? My leg hurts too much for me to sleep, so I worked out an answer for her. Now, put all this junk back where it belongs."

"Yes," she said, and shifted it all away from his bed.

"And now..." he said, and crooked a finger at her. "Over here."

"Not me," she said. "If I were in the Sudan—"

"Don't kid yourself," he said, but there was a wide grin on his face. "They couldn't get you in the Sudan with a pair of elephants pushing and pulling."

"You think I'm a coward, don't you? Well, I'm not. I'm not afraid of the Sudan, or you—well, maybe elephants."

"Prove it. Come over here."

Don't be a fool, she told herself. Stop! But her feet were carrying her—very slowly—in his direction. By the exercise of maximum control she managed to stop a step or two from the bed.

"Look me in the eye," he commanded. "You *are* going to marry me." He had lowered his voice, down into a soft, deep, hypnotic bass. But Hope Latimore was not about to be hypnotized. She mustered up just a shade more strength.

"The hell you say," she managed, quoting her brother's favorite saying. "What do you want for breakfast?"

"Good Lord, surely you're not going to make my breakfast dressed like that?" He grinned—or perhaps it was a leer—and licked his lips. His eyes were focused on a point just under her chin.

Hope stared at him for a moment, then looked slowly down at herself. The only light in the room came from the big table lamp behind her. She was wearing one of her most comfortable nightgowns—a semi-transparent shorty gown that ended just above her knees, and started just below the middle of her very healthy breasts. And the light, of course, outlined her lush figure completely.

"Damn you," she muttered as she fled from the sickroom to the kitchen, where an oversized apron rescued her and restored her dignity. Just in time. She could hear his crutches clomping down the hall, and there he was, with a sheepish smile on his face. She froze in the middle of the room; he stomped around the kitchen table and sat down in one of the cushioned chairs.

"It's been a hard night," he said, sighing. "But I'm glad to get that job done. Life just seems to be full of troubles, doesn't it?"

"Most of them we make for ourselves," she commented as she turned toward the stove. The electric percolator had been filled and plugged in the night before, and now it ceased to bubble and the red light came on.

"Coffee?"

"Yes."

Hope stretched up to the shelf where his mug was stored, filled it almost full, added a drop or two of skimmed milk, and set it down in front of him. "Pancakes?"

"You bet. Got any more of that Portuguese sausage?"

"Linguíça?"

"You bet. And three or four pieces of toast."

She turned around to the stove and began the work. The telephone at his elbow rang. He answered it, and caught her attention at the same time. "Yes," he said. "This is the Browne home, and yes, I'm Ralph Browne. Western Union? A telegram? From—the State

Department? You mean the State Department of the United States, like in Washington DC? Dear Lord, I don't know anyone in the State Department. Yes, read it to me, and then you can mail me a copy."

The prepackaged pancakes were already finished. The sausage was close behind. Hope looked over her shoulder. He was holding the telephone in one hand, away from his ear, and there was something glistening in his eye. A tear? Men didn't cry. Did they?

Hope turned slowly around. "What?" she asked.

"Eloise," he murmured. "My sister Eloise. And her husband Harry."

"The children's parents?"

"Yes." A sober, somber voice. Almost as if he were a thousand miles away.

"In Sanjeet," he added. "Damn. Harry had arranged for a three-month holiday so Eloise could recuperate. The lakes in the Vale of Sanjeet are some of the most beautiful in the world, but there's trouble between Sanjestan and Malikstan about which country owns the area. So, Harry arranged to join a tourist flight over the lakes. And somebody forced the plane down! Sixteen tourists are being held as hostages. Including both Harry and Eloise. My Lord, Eloise has been so sick for so long, and then the minute she gets better—and we don't even know who has them captive. So they won't be home by Easter. What am I going to tell the kids?"

Hope stared at him. There had been all sorts of incidents among Latimore Incorporated employees, but not since Mattie Latimore's troubles in the Sudan had there been a hostage-taking. "I have no idea," she said. "No idea. It might be best not to tell Melody anything. And as for Eddie, he's a pretty mature boy, but I think maybe we shouldn't tell him anything either until he brings up a question about them."

"I've told you all I know," Ralph said. "Or rather all that the State Department knows. I don't have any other relatives. The children will have to stay with me, of course. I don't know if I have enough brains to take care of them." He took a sip from his coffee mug. The coffee was cold. He set the mug back onto the table and reached down for his crutches. It was a difficult moment, struggling to his feet.

"I can help with the children. I don't have any time limit on how long I work here." *With you*, she thought. Ralph was still struggling to get back on his feet. "Now where are you going?"

"I don't know," he said. "I've got to go off and think. Watch the kids for me."

"I can do that." He was the sort of patient who didn't want help getting up, so she didn't offer any. He was an independent man. As are all the Latimores, she thought. And then an idea struck her. "Ralph?"

He turned around. "What?"

"What we need is more information."

"Sure. What would you suggest? We should set up our own undercover spy force?" He shook his head and gave her a sardonic smile.

"It's not all that silly. Latimore's did just that when our men were trapped in Iran. We brought them out safely. We've got a big company, Ralph."

"We?"

"Of course. All of us Latimores have a piece of the action. I wouldn't be surprised to find out that we have teams working in Sanjeet. I know we have groups in Pakistan, and Nepal and— Why don't I...?"

"Yeah, how about that?" He dropped back into the chair, dropped his crutches on the floor, and passed her the telephone. "Who are you going to call?"

"Well, Dad does the specialty work, Mattie does the engineering, and Michael runs the corporation."

"So Michael?"

"Heck, no. I'm going straight to the top. I'm going to call my mother."

Mary Kate Latimore welcomed her call with a typically soft chuckle. "I'm glad to hear from you, sweetheart. As it happens Becky just came in a few minutes ago. She plans to come by and pick up that patient of yours. She wants new X-rays. But that isn't what you called about, is it?"

"No, Mama." Hope explained it all in detail.

"Ah. You want me to fiddle around in the company? What do you suppose Michael will say?"

Hope laughed. "After you explain it all carefully, ne'll be more than willing to help. After all he is your baby."

"You, missy, are getting altogether too sophisticated for this world. What did you say their names were?"

"Jakowski. Harry and Eloise Jakowski. Do you· -?"

"Of course I can check," Mary Kate affirmed. ·'I'd be surprised if we didn't have someone in the area. And how is Mr Browne?"

Hope lowered her voice. "He's well, considering. He's a terrible patient but a wonder with these children. Do you remember him from my high-school days?"

"I remember him well, dear. For a time I thought I might have to do something drastic to or with him. But, you know, he came to the house, explained it all, and apologized as nicely as ever a young man can."

"Secrets?" Ralph struggled back to his feet. 'I'm going out on the porch for a minute or two."

"That'll be nice," Hope said.

"What will be?" her mother asked.

"I—I was talking to Ralph," Hope stammered. "He was—he said he was going outside for a minute."

"So," her mother said, "you called about the missing couple. Was that the only reason you called?"

"Of course not, Ma. I wanted to ask you another question."

"So ask away."

"He—he keeps asking me to marry him. What do you think?"

"Well, now. Of course, you're younger than your sisters were when they got married. And much younger than I was when I walked down the aisle. But what do *you* think?"

Hope hesitated. "I don't know. Sometimes he scares me."

"Oh? You mean he threatens you? Beats up on you?"

"N-no, nothing like that. He—kisses me, and sometimes he says things that are—sort of... And he likes to touch me."

"Sex rears its ugly head?" her mother queried, laughing.

"I—yes."

"Listen, child, sex in marriage is a very nice thing. Very enjoyable. And he's good with children, you say?"

"Very good."

"And you like children yourself?"

"You know I do."

"I must have forgotten," Mary Kate said, laughing. "I know I talked to all your sisters, and I guess I forgot to tell you. Look, Becky is just about to come over to your place now. I'll come with her, and while she takes him out for his X-rays you and I will have a little talk. All right?"

"I'm glad you're my mother," Hope said. "I think I'm going to cry."

"You haven't done a lot of that lately," her mother said. "Well, that will give me time to talk to people about Sanjeet." And then, as an afterthought, she said, "A little crying can sometimes be good for a woman." And she hung up just as Ralph clomped back into the house.

"So what did she say?" he asked.

"She said she would look into it for us."

"And that made you cry?"

"No. She also said—" Hope pulled up her apron to dry her tears.

"You'd better get dressed," he suggested, with a grin on his face. "Although I like to look at girls in shorty nightgowns."

Hope looked down at herself and wailed. Pulling up her apron had displayed far more of herself than she was accustomed to showing. "She also said that you were a nice boy, and I don't understand why she would say that!"

And with that she was gone, heading up the stairs, muttering under her breath.

"Now, that I don't understand," Ralph muttered as he picked up his cold coffee mug. "I *am* a nice boy—er—man."

Upstairs Hope Latimore stalked into her bedroom and slammed the door behind her. She walked over to stand in front of her wall mirror. "Hope Latimore," she snarled at her mirror image, "you are never, ever going to cry again while you're in this house. You hear?"

CHAPTER EIGHT

THE April winds dipped and curtsied among the blossoming trees outside the house. Up in her room Hope heard car noises in the driveway. She ducked into the bathroom, washed her face, and glared at herself in the mirror. The pert little face glared back. "You will not," she lectured herself again, "do any more crying in this house. Understood?" After the nod of agreement she started downstairs at high speed, and met her mother at the door.

"No need to run," Mary Kate Latimore told her youngest daughter. "They've left for the hospital."

"Come and have some coffee," Hope invited. "Everything's out of order around here, but the kids have had breakfast and—"

The computer buzzer went off. Two pairs of little feet pounded down the stairs behind her. Little elephant feet. Hope snatched up Eddie's lunch bag and urged her mother away from the door for safety's sake.

"G'bye, Aunty," the boy yelled, and he snatched the bag, kissed Hope's cheek, stared at Mary Kate for a surprised second, and was gone out the door.

"Eddie," Hope reminded her mother.

"And this is—Melody?"

"I are," the little girl said as she jumped off the third stair, arms outstretched, and landed in Hope's arms. More by good catching than by skillful aiming, it must be said.

"Hope be very good at catchin'." The child chortled. "I learned her."

131

"Practice makes perfect," Hope said solemnly. The three of them started out for the kitchen.

"Hope used to be a pretty good jumper herself," Mary Kate said. "Of course her father was a much bigger target."

"And a darned sight better catcher," Hope avowed as she poured orange juice for the little girl and coffee for her mother.

Melody gulped down her orange juice and stared at Mary Kate. "Hope is my mama," she said firmly, as if expecting someone to deny it.

"And I am Hope's mother." Mary Kate leaned forward and flashed that famous smile of hers that almost always caught children's attention.

The child looked back and forth between the two, and then smiled. "Everybody gotta have a mama," she said. And just at that moment the computer buzzed again. Melody slipped out of her chair. "'Scuse me. I gotta do my homework."

Mary Kate sipped at her coffee, as if remembering. "Homework?"

"Well, it worked for me."

"Ah. I was wondering how we were going to have this—talk—with the little girl around."

"One hour. Fire away."

"First things first, love. The children love you. You've come a long way, my dear. You seem—more adult now than you were just months ago. But the little girl calls you Mama?"

"Just recently. I don't know what brought it on. But lately it's been Mama more often than Aunty. Is that wrong?"

"She's very young, Hope, and she has obviously adopted you, bag and baggage. What happens when her real mother comes home?"

"I—I don't know, Ma. I think it may be just a passing fancy. Nobody taught her to call me Mother. And her brother Eddie doesn't. You know, she's barely three years old, and her mother has been sick and away for so long— almost a year—it just seemed to happen."

"I know. There's no blame attached. But you need to be careful. But that's not what I came to discuss. Let's get S.E.X. out of the way and worry about little girls later, shall we?"

Mary Kate took a deep breath, and started out. "Once upon a time there was a big oak stump from the Liberty Tree in our front yard, and a big man came calling..."

And so it went, the story of the courtship of Mary Kate Chase by Bruce Latimore. About every three or four minutes Hope would interject, "You didn't!" or, "He did?" or, "No, my dad did that?" or, "Mama, you made out like a bandit!" until an hour had passed, and a very much better informed Hope Latimore knew more than she had ever dreamed about the way of a man with a maid—or, in Mary Kate's case, with a widow.

"And that's the way it was," Hope's mother concluded gently. "And then we were married."

The kitchen buzzer went off again. Little feet thundered down the stairs and disappeared into the downstairs bathroom.

"Potty training," Hope told her confused mother. "Do you really think I should marry him?"

"You have to decide that for yourself," her mother said. "Love is a lot of different things for different people. But, if you take him, take him for what he is, not what you think you might make him into. The only one you can change is yourself. Has he asked you?"

"Yes. More than once. And I think..."

"Yes, you think?"

"I think if he asks me again I'll gráb for the brass ring."

Her mother reached over and patted her hand. "Give us a little time. I'm sure all your sisters would like to be at the wedding."

"And Dad?"

"I don't have to *ask* him, my dear. I'll just *tell* him." They both sat back and smiled at each other. In that crowded kitchen it was a woman's world.

"Wedding?" Melody asked as she came back into the room, tugging at her jeans. Neither of the adults had heard her come into the kitchen. "You is gonna get married?"

Hope looked over at her mother, sighed, and shrugged. "Perhaps," she said. "But it has to be a secret, you know. So don't tell anybody, especially your uncle Ralph."

"I can keep a secret," Melody replied, sounding a little hurt. "Well, maybe I can. As long as you ain't gonna marry Uncle Ralph. And what are we gonna do this morning, Mama?"

"Bread," Hope said. "You uncle eats homemade bread as if all the bakeries had gone out of style."

"Funny! Ain't she funny?" Melody giggled, and then remembered something as she stared at Mary Kate. "You is really Hope's mama?"

"Really, truly."

"'An you must be my gramma!"

"Sort of," Mary Kate answered hesitantly. "I'm gramma to a lot of little people. Hope," she cautioned, "you'd better be careful with this line of work. Suppose—when Eloise comes back...?"

"I won't forget," Hope said, "but I don't really know how to go about making a change."

"Who doesn't know what?" came a strong baritone voice from the area of the front door just as Becky came in. Ralph was behind her, walking with a cane, but without crutches or cast.

"Uncle Ralph," Melody yelled as she raced across the kitchen and jumped up at him. "You're all better?"

"I believe I am," he said, catching her in midair.

"But not too much of this acrobatic stuff," Becky warned. "At least for a few weeks more. Ready to go, Ma?"

"I believe so," Mary Kate agreed. "I've had a nice talk with Hope, and a nice talk with Melody." She struggled up out of her chair, not as agile as she once had been.

"An' I know a secret," Melody yelled. "I gotta whisper, 'cos it's a secret."

"Right in my ear," Uncle Ralph directed.

"Oh, no," Hope groaned.

"Hope's gonna get married! I told ya you'd wait too long!"

Her uncle, holding the child in his arms, turned to look at Hope. His eyes were as hard as flint; the grin had gone. "Really?"

"Really," his little niece said excitedly.

"Goodbye," Mary Kate said as she took Becky's arm and tugged her toward the door.

"Cowards," Hope muttered.

"Little pitchers, love." Her mother grinned at her and reached for the door.

Becky looked back at her youngest sister, hesitated, shrugged, and followed her mother out the door.

"I think," Uncle Ralph said, "that you shouldn't have told me your secret, Melody."

*   *   *

It was afternoon before things settled down again and Melody went off for her nap. Ralph was moving aimlessly around in what had been his sickroom for so long when Hope gathered up her courage and went in, bringing him another cup of coffee.

"Thanks a lot," he acknowledged, without looking at her. "I'm—we're going to miss you around here."

Hope was wearing a skirt and blouse, with a little bow tie to match. She swept her skirts under her and collapsed in his big easy chair. "Oh?"

"Well, you've been here for some time—"

"Are you firing me?"

"Me? Fire you? Don't be silly! But you can't expect your new husband to let you continue like this."

"I can't?"

"Of course you can't. Who is it? That guy your brother brought around?"

"Alfred?" And would you care if it was? she wondered. She cocked her head and stared at him. Not a muscle in his face moved. Not a millimeter. If he cares, it can't be very much! she thought. "No. I would rather go into a convent than marry Alfred." And then there was another moment of silence. "And I hate the idea of convents."

For the first time he looked over at her and cleared his throat. "Somebody I might know?"

He still doesn't care, Hope told herself. He's just making conversation. She licked her upper lip, a nervous childhood habit she had never overcome. She shrugged.

"You might know him. He's from around town."

"Well, that's good. It's always best to marry someone you know. And his family too, I suppose."

"Yes," she agreed, "I suppose." But by that time he had picked up the morning paper and begun to thumb through to the sports page. Hope came to her feet. He stirred not a bit, except for his eyes, which shuttled back and forth on the page in front of him and occasionally flashed in her direction.

"I might as well get supper going," she muttered. Not a sound from Ralph, not even a twitch of his paper. Hope took a step toward the door. Her neck was stiff from concentrating on him. To no avail. She shook her long blonde hair until it swirled around her neck. Then she stiffened her back and walked, head high, out of the room. She had not yet reached the kitchen door when something in the sickroom crashed enthusiastically into something else. Hope automatically ducked her head.

"Is something wrong?" she called back down the corridor.

"Hell, no," he growled back at her. "How could anything be wrong? I—dropped my watch."

"I'll bet you did," she muttered as she entered the kitchen, and went over to the table and flipped her recipe book open to the chapter on quiches. She might have put one on the menu had it not been for the children. Not for the life of her would she make another quiche and try to get the kids to eat it. So the answer was simple—hamburgers.

Eddie came home from school at about that time, celebrating his return with a cowboy yell, and skidding his books down the slippery floor of the ground-floor corridor. "Anybody home?"

Hope rushed to the kitchen door to shush him. Melody was at her nap, and maybe the lord of the manor had settled down for forty winks. At least it could be fervently hoped that he had.

The boy made a show of it, stopping abruptly and then proceeding down the corridor to the kitchen on his toes. "Uncle Ralph too?"

"Uncle Ralph too."

"I'm hungry."

"When are you not hungry? Did you eat that lunch I packed for you?"

"I ate it all. Usually I trade among the kids, but today it was so good that I ate every stitch of it. What do ya have for nibbling?"

"Cookies, in the jar. Milk."

"I don't know how we ever got along without you," he commented as he stuffed both hands down into the ceramic cookie jar.

"Me neither." She grinned shamelessly at him.

And with both hands loaded with chocolate chip cookies he paused just long enough to kiss her cheek, and then went off up the stairs, precariously balancing the glass of milk under his elbow.

So there, she told herself. Both the children love me. But that—Uncle Ralph—I ought to—

The telephone rang, interrupting her rage. She snatched at it in the middle of the first ring. Had she let it ring one more time the old grouch would have been down on her like Attila the Hun!

"Hello? Hope Latimore here."

"Ms Latimore, this is Peter Foster from the Latimore communications room."

Her mind went into high gear. Not only was he in the communications room but he was also the young man in charge of all the codes and ciphers. "Yes, Peter?"

"I have a curious message from our man in Geetan."

Geetan? Her mind fumbled with it. Geography had never been her most favored subject. She worked up a cough to cover the embarrassing pause.

"In Sanjestan," he prompted.

"Yes, of course. Can you read it to me?"

"I can read it to you, ma'am, but it's not in any of the house codes, and I don't know what it means."

"Go ahead, Peter."

He began slowly, reciting a string of numbers that meant less than nothing to Hope. Until near the end he switched to letters. "H.L.," he said. "Query G.O."

"Peter, I'll have to call you back. Do you have faith in Geetan Station?"

"Our best man is out there, ma'am. He's the one who arranged for our people to get out of Iran some years ago. I'll wait for your call."

"How long can you wait?"

"How long? As long as it takes, Miss Hope. I've worked for your father for ten years now. Call when you can. I'll be by the telephone."

She hung up the telephone, thinking. Ralph must be consulted. And then Michael. And maybe even Pa? But Ralph to begin with.

She picked up her scribbled notes and went to the table in her bedroom. Numbers? H.L.? Hope Latimore, of course. And the numbers. The lowest number one, the highest twenty-two. And who in chronograph knew the private family code? A simple code. Each number stood for one letter, inverted in the alphabet system. The code that she and Michael had constructed in their childhood. How old could "our man in Geetan" be? Something to think of later. For now, the English translation...

The message grew slowly under her eyes, until it was all spread out before her.

Plane forced down sixteen miles from Geetan by Stinger missiles. Passengers alive but some injuries. Both Jakowskis in fair shape. Captors minor guerrilla force from a former Communist group. Demand one million pounds British for all captives. All passengers employees of Latimore's. Have little trust in captors. Military help available from Geetan. Query Go?

Hope took a deep breath. The pound was exchangeable at one point sixty-one cents on the week's market quotations. That meant roughly one million six hundred thousand dollars in ransom. She wrote the whole thing down, gulped at the cost, shrugged, and went down the hall. Ralph was coiled up on his bed in a fetal position.

"Ralph?"

He unwound himself and sat up on the bed. "More Latimore tricks?"

"I suppose you might call it that. This message is just in from Geetan, Sanjestan." She passed the notes over and Ralph scanned them.

"I—er—can't quite make out your handwriting. Could you tell me instead?"

"Sure. They have found the airplane where it was forced down by Stinger missiles. American missiles. We left a lot of them behind in that area. Most of the survivors, including the Jakowskis, are in good shape. They are all in the hands of guerrillas, who are holding them hostage for one million six hundred thousand dollars—"

Ralph interrupted with a fine whistle. "That's a lot of money."

"Yeah, that's true, but we've paid more than that in other places. Two of them are your family, after all, and the others are all employees. We have a standard rule in the company, Ralph. We always bring our own back home. And notice that this site is sixteen miles over the Malikstan border. And maybe we can get it done cheaper. Probably half a million, using some of our Malikstan friends. Mind you, Michael has the final say, but we need everybody else to contribute. What say you?"

"What are you saying?"

"These guerrillas are not to be trusted. We either ransom them out or we send in a force and take them out, or we do nothing at this time and take the risk of losing them all."

"Hey, those are tough words, lady. You're suggesting we organize our own army?"

"Not exactly organize. Rent our own army, rather. And Latimore Incorporated has done it before. Or shall we leave them all in the hands of the guerrillas and hope for the best?"

"I'm not much for the diplomatic approach, but our own army..."

"Fish or cut bait," Hope snapped.

"Yeah, well," he said, sighing. "Anything except the diplomats. Why is it that I thought of you as the soft, sweet type?"

"I used to be—but I don't intend to stand short while Melody's real mother is having such—"

"All right," he said, throwing up his hands. "What do we do next?"

"First we call my brother Michael."

"And then?"

"And then we'll see."

"And so we will," he said. "How about a kiss?"

He was moving, crab-like, in her direction. She lifted a hand and made a halt signal.

"No kisses?"

"I'm the girl who's going to get married," she reminded him. And if you don't know to whom it serves you right, she thought. Tell me that you love me and we'll see what kissing is all about!

And once again the pride of the Browne family flunked his test. "Ah, yes, getting married, aren't you?" And he settled back on the bed for a second, and then moved away from her.

"Let's call Michael," she finally suggested. He picked up the telephone and did just that. Michael was away in the depths of Venezuela.

"So call Pa." He did. And when he put the phone down there was an expression of desperation on his face.

"Your father has just this afternoon taken your mother to the Judicial Convention in Hawaii. They won't be back for a week. Didn't she mention it to you this morning? And your sister Mattie, the chief engineer, is still in Africa. Lord, don't any of your family stay at home?"

Hope vaguely remembered her mother mentioning the convention a while back. It had completely slipped her mind.

But she could hardly stand around twiddling her thumbs when Ralph's family was in such trouble. Her sister Becky had withdrawn from the corporate management when she'd passed her medical exams. Her sister Faith was down in the Caribbean. So? "Well, there's always me," Hope said.

"You?" Well, he didn't have to sound so disgusted about it, she thought. This man had a lot to learn about the Latimore family!

"Yes, me. I'm a vice-president of the corporation too, you know. So give me the darn phone." He did. She dialed. "Peter? Hope Latimore." Not being a complete fool, she put more emphasis on the Latimore than on the Hope. "Pass the word to our man in Geetan. The answer is Go." And she hung up the phone, utterly satisfied with herself.

It was hard not to laugh at the expression on Ralph's face. "Over a million-five," he said in awe. "Just like that?"

"Just like that," she told him. "Maybe it'll come in a little cheaper, or maybe they'll accept something on the installment plan."

"Yeah, and maybe it'll come in at twice that much."

"Maybe, but it isn't your money and it *is* your sister. Now how about some dinner?"

There was something heady about being a Latimore, Hope told herself as she set the hamburgers on to be flame-broiled. From millions to hamburgers? Well, it was worth the effort. Once when she was seventeen and up to her ears in environmental protection she had become so incensed with a Latimore highway construction through the Berkshires that she had called in to the corporate operations office and ordered the entire contract to a halt. And had then hidden in the closet when her father had come home some five days later.

And all he had said, with a solemn face, was, "Prove it." So she had screwed up her courage and, to an audience of her father and mother and brother Michael, had done just that. As a result of which the highway had been stopped halfway to New York, and made into a parkland trail. And little Hope Latimore had been appointed chief of the Latimore environmental office. And had never since tried to exercise her authority again—until today, that was.

The computer buzzer sounded off in her ears, the children clattered down from upstairs, and a glum adult voice said in her ear, "I don't think we want the hamburgers to be as black as—"

"Oh, shut up," Hope said as she reached for the spatula and rescued the dinner.

"Oh, shut up? Getting a little too courageous, aren't we?" They were standing nose to nose. He leaned over and dropped a kiss on the center of her forehead, and laughed as she snorted in disgust at him.

"Taking advantage," she snarled at him. "If I didn't have my hands full you wouldn't—"

He repeated the process on one of her blushing cheeks, and aimed for the other.

She pushed him aside and moved the platter to the table, put both hands on her hips, and glared at him. "As I remember it, your doctor said you should be very cautious about that leg of yours. Not being a medical person, I suspect that a good swift kick in the right place would take care of your problem." She made a threatening movement with her left foot.

He backed away. "Hey, I was only kidding."

"I'll bet you were. Sit!"

He sat.

The children arrived. "Why so quiet?" Eddie asked as he came in from the bathroom.

"Meditation," Hope told him. "Your uncle and I were just—meditating."

"Like saying a prayer?"

"Something like that."

"Like what?" Melody popped into the room, a big smile on her face.

"Did you?" her aunt asked.

"Course I did. I ain't no dummy." The child held out both hands, dripping water all over the floor.

"Of course you ain't—aren't," Hope responded as she used her apron to trap the hands and dry them off. "You've even got me talking that way. Give us a kiss, and then up to the table, girl."

"Yes, Mama."

Over the child's head Hope looked at Ralph and saw the frown on his face. She shrugged and gave him a "What can I do?" look. He shook his head and raised both hands halfway in a "Beats me" gesture. So Hope snatched up the child, hugged and kissed her, and set her in her place at the table. It wasn't easy. Melody Jakowski was getting to be a very weighty little girl.

"Hamburgers," Melody shouted. "What a good mama you is."

"But only if you eat your green salad," Hope said.

"She ain't your mama," Eddie piped up. "She ain't even your aunty. In fact, she ain't nothing connected to us."

Melody put down her milk glass, slowly and gently, but she looked as if she wanted to throw it at her brother. "You is a bad boy, Eddie," she said mournfully. "Of course she is my mother."

"Is not!"

"Is. Uncle Ralph, ain't she?"

"Well, I really—" He stopped in mid-sentence. "I'm afraid I can't say," he said apologetically.

"Is," Melody insisted. "Is. Ain't you, Hope?"

"I think your uncle is a coward," Hope responded. "He's your mother's brother, you know. If he can't say, how could I?" She leaned across the table to brush a tear from the child's eye. "But if you want me to be your mother for a while I don't mind."

"So there," Melody sneered at Eddie.

The boy sneered back at her. "Well, she ain't *my* mother," he muttered. "So if she's your mother and not mine, then I ain't your brother, am I?" And he returned to his hamburger, and after a bite or two did something he had never done before. He snatched a few leaves of lettuce from his salad and nibbled on it as if he really liked salad.

This time when Melody picked up her milk glass everyone else at the table ducked. But she only sipped at it and then glared at her brother.

"Hope are my mother," the little girl said. "I want her to be my mother. And if you ain't my brother I don't care." At which point two things happened at once. Tears began to cascade from her big, bright eyes, and the rest of the milk spilt out across the table, hitting both Eddie and Uncle Ralph in equal proportions.

Eddie sputtered and scraped back out of his chair. "I don't need no girl for a sister," he roared, and, as big a boy as he was, he too started to cry.

"Well, I'm glad," Melody screamed at him. "I don't need no brother. And I don't need no uncle either." With which she slid off her chair and stomped to the door.

"Mind your manners," Uncle Ralph commanded. Melody glared at him.

"Y-yes, sir," she stammered through her tears. "'Scuse me." And she dashed for the stairs.

"I'll go up with her," Hope offered. "Every girl needs a mother."

"Whoever told you that was lying," Uncle Ralph growled. "You haven't eaten any of your dinner. You sit there. *I'll* go up to her."

"Don't you dare lay a hand on her," Hope snapped at him.

Ralph Browne got up slowly, wiping the side of his face with his napkin. Milk on his cheek, and a cluster of hamburger and ketchup from his lips. "I've never hit a female in my life," he said. "But a few more remarks from you and I might change my habits." He stalked out of the room.

"Wow," Eddie said as he stifled his tears.

"Whatever happened to us?" Hope asked.

"Don't worry none," Eddie said as he pushed his chair around next to Hope's. "She's only a baby. Don't *you* start crying now."

"Oh, I won't," Hope said as she furtively stabbed at her eye—the one on the side furthest away from the boy. Eddie climbed up into his chair and put his arms around her.

"You know what?"

Hope looked down at him. "No, I don't know what."

"I miss my mom and my dad," he said, hugging her tightly. "I 'magine Melody does too. They been gone a long time."

"Yes, I understand. I miss my mom and dad when they're away someplace. But they always come back."

"You mean my—they'll come back?"

"Bound to," she told him, and wished that she could be sure of it.

At that moment Ralph came down the stairs, shaking his head.

"How is she?" Hope asked.

"I don't know," he said, sighing. "She cried for a while, demanded that I acknowledge that you are her mother, and then she fell asleep."

"She's a good kid, but she don't know nothin'," Eddie stated. "When Mom gets home she'll be all right; you'll see."

Uncle Ralph patted him on the shoulder. "If you stick with her she's bound to be all right," he said.

"Ain't no trouble. I like her." He moved closer to Hope and put one of his arms around her. "And we all like you, Aunty Hope."

* * *

That night Hope Latimore went up the stairs as if she were floating on a cloud. And Ralph Browne, for some strange reason, stood at the foot of the stairs and watched her, every step of the way.

CHAPTER NINE

A MONTH passed, fitful April turning into glorious May. Grass plaited the side of the hill in front of and behind the house, fighting a battle with the dandelions. Hope opened all the windows—except for the attic few in Ralph's workroom—which no one dared to touch. Eddie, grown another inch or two, tried out for the B-level Little League and won a spot on the Bears. And Melody, changed from a cheerful three-year-old to a glum one, followed Hope around the house, clinging to her skirts whenever strangers appeared.

And on May the second a telegram arrived from Geetan. All it said was, "Bingo."

Eight days later, while Ralph was upstairs communing with gigabytes, Eddie was off at baseball practice, and Hope was vacuuming the living room, a car drove up to the house. A moment or two later the front doorbell rang. Already standing at the door, Hope clicked off the switch on the noisy machine and opened the screen door.

"Yes?"

The woman was about five feet seven, dressed in the newest spring styles, but with a worn face and tired eyes. Her dark brown hair was a match for Eddie's. She seemed surprised to see Hope. "This is—Ralph Browne's house?"

"It is," Hope replied, "but he's working at the computer. We make it a practice never to disturb him when he's up there. Besides, he locks the door when he's hot on the trail of something, and the door's locked, so I suppose—"

"I understand. Is that Melody?" The girl was standing on the third stair, one thumb in her mouth. "She was only a baby when I last saw her. Come to Mama, baby."

"You ain't my mama," Melody roared as she jumped down the stairs and clutched at the back of Hope's skirt. "Hope is my mama."

"Oh, dear Lord," Hope murmured. "Eloise?"

The woman in front of her nodded. Hope opened her arms and hugged her.

"She *ain't* my mama," the little girl muttered, and clutched at Hope's skirts even tighter. "She *ain't!*"

"Now, now," Hope soothed. "I'm sorry—Eloise. I'm Hope Latimore, Ralph's housekeeper. You can see we've developed a problem. Are you all right?"

"Me? I'm well, but Harry— In all the confusion when the men came to rescue us, Harry was shot in the foot. They took him from Logan airport directly to Deaconess Hospital in Boston. It's not a serious problem but they wanted X-rays and things like that, and I wanted to see the children so badly, so I—so that nice man Peter something or other who met me at the airport leased a car for me and I drove down directly. Peter— Latimore? Are you the one? He said one of the Latimore family had arranged everything!"

Let's hope nobody else hears from Peter, Hope thought. "Yes, I'm the one. But only because I happened to be the only Latimore at home, you see. I'm not the most important Latimore in the world. Come in, Eloise, and sit. You must be worn out with all that traveling."

"Well, young lady, as far as Harry and I are concerned, you're the most important Latimore in the world. And Eddie? How is Eddie?"

"Eddie is in fine shape. He's over at the Little League field practicing. I expect he'll be along in a few minutes."

"She's not my mama," Melody muttered, and then, louder, "*You* is—are my mother, Hope."

Hope sat down in the big rocking chair and gathered the little girl in her arms. "Now, love, I know it's hard for you to understand, but it's not really true. I came here when Eloise, your real mother, had to go away for a while, but I was only your temporary mother. Now Eloise is back, ready to take over the job, and she's brought your father back with her. Pretty soon you'll be going with both of them back to your own home. She *is* your mother, you know."

The thumb went back into Melody's mouth. She shook her head negatively, and snuggled tight up against Hope's chest.

"Well, I guess this is a big enough emergency, Eloise. Do you see that little white button on the arm of your chair? Give it a push, will you?"

"This one?"

"That one."

With more emphasis than was necessary Eloise depressed the white button. Out in the kitchen something clicked in the little computer hanging on the wall, and then all the bells in the house began a clatter that even woke Rex up. The old dog came sliding down the stairs at an angle, spotted the interloper, and managed to work up a husky, but not too threatening bark.

Melody raised her head and watched the dog. She trusted the big animal. Obviously if the dog approved of this stranger, then—

Rex, like an old stage performer, strolled around the two occupied chairs, stopped long enough to sniff at Eloise, then sat down in front of her and lowered his big body down across Eloise's shoes. It was a sure sign of canine approval. Melody pulled her thumb out of her mouth, and was about to say something when Eddie banged into the house, skidded his catcher's glove down the hall, and gave a little whoop. "Aunty Hope," he yelled, "I hit a home run, and I—" His eyes strayed to the opposite chair. For a second he seemed confused, and then his eyes lit up.

"Mama!" he roared as he dashed across the room and threw himself into Eloise's lap. "Mama!"

"Well, he don't know nuffin'," his sister sneered. "He's only a boy."

"Me too," said the baritone voice from the middle of the stairs. "Hello, Eloise, it's good to see you." And Ralph Browne came down the stairs two at a time, swept his sister up in his arms, and twirled her around the room. Rex, seeing a new game in this, followed them around, barking. Hope, watching the reunion, got up from her chair and got out of the way, a big smile on her face. Eddie let it all proceed for a moment or two, and then stepped in their way and forced a halt.

"That's *my* mama," the boy said. He had grown a lot, both physically and mentally.

"I know," his uncle admitted as he relinquished his hold. "She's *your* mama but she's still *my* sister." He ruffled the boy's close-cut hair and stepped out of the way.

"No, she ain't," Melody muttered as she backed up against Hope and maintained her defiant attitude.

Hope dropped a hand onto each of the child's narrow shoulders. "Did you ever stop to think," she coaxed, "that you might have *two* mothers?"

"Two mothers? That's a lot."

"It is that. Why don't you go and give your first mother a hug?"

"First mother?" Melody pulled her thumb out of her mouth, slid off Hope's lap and down to the floor.

"Of course," Eloise said. "Why didn't I think of that?" She held out her arms and Melody, convinced at last, ran across the room and climbed up into her lap.

There was quiet for a moment. Even Rex flopped down on his stomach and watched.

"Now, what we need—" Hope started to say, but Eddie interrupted.

"Is pizza," the boy said.

"And why didn't *I* think of that?" Hope exclaimed as she got up and started for the kitchen. Everyone followed along.

They gathered around the table, all five of them. "S'good," Melody said as she sank her teeth into her third slice of pizza.

"Better 'n good," Eddie insisted. "Nobody can cook as good as Hope can. I mean—"

"I agree with you," Eloise commented as she started on her second slice. "No wonder Melody didn't want to give up her second mother."

"Well, maybe you could learn," Eddie suggested. "Maybe you could come over afternoons and take lessons?"

"Not a chance," Uncle Ralph chimed in. "In case you don't know it, your aunt and I are going to get married PDQ."

"What's that mean—PDQ?" Melody asked.

"It means pretty darn quick," her brother explained. "But I still don't see why we couldn't—"

"Because I don't share," Uncle Ralph said very firmly. "This woman is mine. She's been mine since high-school days, and I'm gonna keep her!"

"An' I used to think you was the nicest man in the world," Melody mourned. "I couldn't be more wronger." There was a pause for thought. "An' I won't be able to steal over and sneak some pizza 'cos I'm gonna be in kindergarten next year. What a mean guy you is!''

Hope nudged him under the table. ''The truth finally comes out,'' she whispered. ''Cupboard love.''

''After the wedding you won't be all that independent,'' he returned ominously.

''That's what you think! You haven't heard me say I'll marry you. I'm not that dumb!''

''What are you two arguing about?'' Eloise asked. ''Fighting before the wedding?''

''We just wondered if you want us to pack up all the children's gear and take it over to Myrtle Street tonight,'' Ralph said.

''I'm not sure when Harry will be able to come home from the hospital.'' Eloise looked Ralph up and down suspiciously, and then broke into a wide grin.

''Is that the idea? We'll take our kids away and you two can spend the night smooching?''

''Oh, no,'' Hope gasped. ''My mother wouldn't allow that.''

''Damn your mother,'' Ralph snarled.

''Don't you ever say that about my mother,'' Hope said fiercely as she pushed back her chair and stood up. ''Go ahead; send the children home.''

Ralph leaned over and picked up the telephone. ''Deaconess?''

His sister nodded. He flipped through the telephone book, found the number, and dialed. Moments later he murmured something into the phone and cradled the instrument.

''He's ready to come home,'' Ralph reported. ''Hell, eager to come home. He's in the lobby now, and says if somebody doesn't show up he'll get a cab.''

''Men!'' Eloise shook her head. ''But then he hasn't seen the kids in a long time himself.''

"So, Eloise, we'll all go get him. Hope will pack up the kids' things, I'll drive you all home, and then I'll bring your whole family's goods over to Myrtle Street. Mrs Culbert has been at the house for the past two weeks, and she'll have everything shipshape. Bargain?"

"I'd really love that," his sister said. "When can we go?"

He looked at his huge wristwatch. "Say about ten minutes ago?"

Both the children cheered. "You don't have to push us out," Eloise commented. "Hope?"

Hope blinked to clear her eyes. I will never cry again in this house, she reminded herself. "That would be fine. Children need to be with their parents."

It was like the scattering of a covey of quail. Everyone had a different goal in mind. Everyone was cheering. Except Hope. She manufactured a smile and stationed herself by the front door. Even Rex looked as if he had somewhere to go. He sat on the opposite side of the doorway, his heavy tongue panting up a fire-storm. Gradually the various people clumped down the stairs, carrying light jackets, their faces alight.

"I need to thank you, Hope," Eloise said. "Obviously you've done marvelous things for my children. And for my brother as well." The two exchanged hugs.

"Be back soon," Ralph said as he opened the door for his sister. Rex came up to his feet.

"Not you," Eddie commanded. Rex stood up on his hind legs and licked the boy's nose. "Hey," the boy said, but he was laughing as he dodged that massive tongue and went out the door.

And then it was time for Melody. She had been smiling at the top of the stairs, had a half-grin near the bottom, but when she stepped off onto the floor all traces of her smile were gone. "Oh, Mama Hope," she said, sighing.

Her little eyes were wide and shining. Hope swept her up and squeezed her tightly.

"Don't worry, love. We'll be living in the same town, and you can come to see me whenever you wish."

"But it won't be the same," the girl whispered, very suddenly all grown-up.

"Everything changes," Hope whispered back. "Now give us a kiss and go with your family." She gave her another squeezing hug. The girl complied, but as Hope lowered her to her feet the tears began to run down her round, sweet face, and she stifled a sob as she went out the door. Somebody closed the door behind her. Ralph, Hope thought. And then the door opened again.

"No crying now," Ralph commanded.

"I'm not crying," she said sturdily, "but poor Melody—"

"She'll be all right. She has her whole family to take care of her now." His hand reached out for the doorknob. "And I'll be back in a flash to take care of you."

"And a heck of a lot of good that'll do," she murmured as the door closed behind him. She leaned against it and listened until the car's engine started to rumble. And then she turned and went up the stairs to begin the packing.

And I'm not going to cry in this house again, she promised herself. But it was easy to promise and hard not to cry.

Ralph was true to his word. He was back in a flash. Well, three or four flashes. Three hours, twenty minutes and fourteen seconds, to be exact. But, of course, who was counting?

"Where in the world have you been?" she snapped at him when he came in the door. Rex ducked behind the sofa then ran back up the stairs.

"I'm glad to know you missed me." He came across the room in four strides and swept her up in his arms.

"And that's all you know," she muttered into his ear. And before she could take a deep breath he had her pinned against his muscular shoulder. The kiss lasted for minutes that seemed like hours, and then he let her down to the floor.

"Now why did you do that? My mother would give you what for."

"Yeah, but your mother isn't here, is she?"

"But when I tell her about all this there will be heads flying, believe you me. And besides that I'm going to call Rex and have him raise a little hell around here."

"Now there's a believable threat." He chuckled raucously.

"Now you just wait and see. Rex. *Rex!*" Much to her surprise the big dog was paying attention. First, they could hear his heavy body stirring over their heads. Then there was the thumping as his massive paws hit the stairs, and then they barely had time to turn around, still wrapped in each other's arms, before the dog was in front of them, body close to the floor and enormous teeth shielding a growl.

It had been years since Hope had needed commands for her dog. Most of the time he slumped to the floor and waited to see what would happen. This time he had come to a stiff-legged halt, teeth bared.

"Oh, dear," Hope muttered. "I didn't— Rex, guard! I mean—sit!"

The dog gave her a doubtful look, the animal equivalent of "Make up your mind, lady", and then dropped to a sitting position.

"Would he have?" Ralph asked.

"You'd better believe he would," Hope gasped. "It's been so long that I—forgot the commands."

"Well, thank you, ma'am," Ralph grumbled as he made his way over to the other side of the room. "It's a long time since I've been a meal for an animal. An old animal, at that." Rex came up on his four feet and bared his teeth again.

"And he doesn't like to be called old, you know."

"Oh. So what should I call him?"

"He's sensitive, like people. For some reason he likes to be called puppy. Like this. Rex, sit, puppy." And the massive old dog sat, and stuck his tongue out at them. "See what I mean?"

"It's hard to believe, girl. Hard to believe. We're going to have to do something about him after we marry."

Hope drew herself up to her full five feet. "I don't remember having been asked to marry you," she said bluntly. "And I'm sure if I'd ever been asked I never would have accepted!"

"Poppycock," he snapped. "I know you're going to marry me; *you* know you're going to marry me. Even your mother knows you're going to marry me."

"Now that's what I call real poppycock. How can you know that my mother knows that I'm going to marry you? How?"

"How? Because I asked her, and she agreed it would be a nice thing!"

"You asked my mother but you didn't ask me?"

"That's about it," he admitted humbly. "Kind of dumb, wasn't it?"

"Not *kind of* dumb," Hope said in her most chilly voice. "*Absolutely* dumb! You have just won first prize in the Mr Stupid contest! Why didn't you ask me?"

"That's a good question," he returned, sighing.

"For which you don't have an answer?"

"Oh, I have an answer," he protested. "In fact I have a half-dozen answers. But none of them are what I would call *good* answers. I really thought that I was going to marry you, and then you came up with the flat-out statement that you were going to marry someone else. Now that was a first-class catastrophe. Who?"

"Who what?"

"Who is this guy you think you're going to marry, that's what. Or who, as the case may be. Whom?"

"Ralph Browne, if I hadn't taken the seat in front of you in high-school junior and senior English you might never have graduated."

He shrugged. "It didn't seem to be so important after you transferred to the Catholic high school. I *did* graduate, but only just. Who is the guy?"

"There was never any other guy."

"Never? But who is the guy now? Some fellow you picked up in the construction business?"

"No."

"Dammit, tell me who's the guy you're all wound up with. The guy you told Melody you were going to marry."

She moved slowly and carefully over in front of him, her hands folded behind her, a broad smile on her face. "You, that's who."

She looked so lovably sweet, her face so wonderfully formed—and both hands were fastened behind her, trembling.

"You mean to tell me—" he started to say, but she interrupted.

"Yes."

"You mean—? Dear Lord," he muttered. "You have given me the worst time I've ever had in the last few weeks."

"That's good. A few weeks? That's better than I expected."

Rex stirred fitfully on the floor and then came to his feet. "Rex, go," she commanded, and pointed toward the stairs. "Upstairs, puppy. Time to get your nap." And her loving old mutt gave her a short yap and stalked out, all love and beauty and puzzlement. The pair of them watched until his heavy tail had disappeared around the corner of the stairs. And then they turned to each other and joined hands in the narrow space which separated them.

"You did it on purpose, didn't you?"

"Yes, of course," she told him. "I had to do something, didn't I? You were getting far too dominant. And my mother told me—"

"I might have known," he groaned as he seized her, pulling her close up against him. "Your sweet little mother, right?"

"There's never been one sweeter or better," she teased him. "She knows what's what, my mother." Her hands stole up around his neck and pulled his face down to where her mouth could reach. "When we marry, she's going to be your mother-in-law; did you ever think of that?" And then she kissed him swiftly and sweetly.

He obviously hadn't given Mary Kate a thought, but he did now, and liked everything he thought about. "A girl with a mother like yours could be a lot of fun," he whispered. For a moment he let Hope control the kiss, and then she could feel the fire rising up inside him. He swept her up off her feet, taking the weight of her on his right arm under her knees, and overwhelmed her with his passion. She yielded bravely and willingly.

Moments later he carried her over to the couch and set her down gently on his lap. "Poor little girl," he said.

"Poor little girl?"

"You haven't the slightest idea what's going to happen to you," he said, and produced one of those villainous movie leers.

And I haven't, she told herself, but he shan't know that. Not a bit. "Oh, I know a thing or three," she answered, and then giggled.

"A thing or three? When I get you all married up, my dear, I'm going to stretch you out on my bed and we're going to play a game only married people play... You know what that game is?"

"Don't be silly."

"Oh? Your mother didn't tell you about that game?"

She squirmed away from him, looking around the room for something or someone to come to her aid, then looked back at him, with teeth clenched and eyes sparking. "I don't want to know about any game," she insisted. "Let go of me. Turn me loose, you—you philanderer. Don't you dare put your hands on—"

"Ah, little girl, your ignorance has done you in!"

"If you don't take your hand away I'm going to call my dog and have him—"

"Eat me?"

"What a good idea. We're not married yet, you know, and if you keep on the way you're going there isn't going to be— Don't do that! I don't give samples!"

"I know you don't, love. But let me show you something."

And he did.

CHAPTER TEN

"AND what made you decide to come home?" Mary Kate, Hope's mother, was at the front door of the old Gothic wooden house next to the Episcopal church. She was holding a small trowel in one hand and balancing a pair of potted flowers in the other. Roses, in fact. White roses.

"I thought I'd better," Hope said as she tried to balance on the stone step just below. "The kids went home yesterday."

"Ah. Their parents came home from—where was it?"

"Sanjestan."

"Yes, I remember. I've always wanted to see that place. The most beautiful lakes in the world, they used to say. So the kids went home to—Myrtle Street, was it?"

"Yes."

"And you miss them already?"

"Yes."

"My, what a talkative daughter you've become."

"Yes. I mean—yes."

"I've got to go by the cemetery, love. It's Mr Chase's birthday."

"Mr Chase?"

"Becky's father. And if you say 'Becky who?' we're going straight back into the house and you're going to have a medical stimulant."

"Ma! I remember Becky very well. My oldest sister. The doctor. She married Jake—*married* Jake."

"Ah, there's something fishy about the word 'married', is there? Come along, child. I have a passel of things to do today." Mary Kate came down the last step, passed the trowel to her youngest daughter, took the girl's free hand, and started out behind the church. The little cemetery stretched at some length back there, separated from the house of worship by an iron fence and a row of ancient elm trees. Mrs Bethel, the widow of the former pastor, was trying to open the gate.

"Mary Kate. Just the one. I can't get this gate open."

"I'll get it," Hope said, and squeezed around the pair of them to do just that.

"It must be nice to have children," Mrs Bethel sighed. "Henry and I—we always wanted a good half-dozen, and never had a one."

"But you had a whole parish full of them, Theresa. Hope, Mrs Bethel played the organ for the service when your father and I were married. Right here in this church. And taught Sunday school as well."

"It must have been wonderful, Ma. I—but if Mrs Bethel—I mean—suppose somebody else wanted to get married, and needed someone to play—"

"And there's that word again," Mary Kate said. "Married. I'm sure we could find an organist who could play for a wedding service, couldn't we, Theresa?"

"We had three weddings last Saturday, Mary Kate. No trouble." Both of them turned to stare at Hope in anticipation.

She looked back at them, puzzled. Ralph had told her two disturbing things. First, "Keep your mouth shut." And, second, "A small, quiet wedding." And she didn't agree with either one of the statements.

"I think my baby girl and I have to have a talk," Mary Kate said. "You'll excuse us, Theresa?"

And in a matter of seconds Hope had been dragged through the cemetery gate and down to the back plot where all the Chases were laid to rest. "Put those flowers on either side of the headstone," Mary Kate commanded.

Hope started to dig and read at the same time. "Colonel Henry Chase?" she asked.

Mary Kate looked over at her. "Becky's father," she said. "My first husband."

"But I thought Becky was—"

"My stepdaughter, love. A crazy, mixed-up family, the Chases. And then your father came along and married the whole bunch of us, and we all became Latimores." Mary Kate groaned and clapped a hand to her hip as she stood up and moved over to the nearest iron bench. "I'm not the woman I used to be. Come sit by me. We have something to talk about."

Hope complied cautiously. As the almost-baby of the family she always watched her step when the older folk said, "We have something to talk about." And this was one of those times. And no matter how much silence Ralph had commanded he was a good mile or so down the road, and Mary Kate was right here.

"What do you suppose we have to talk about?" she asked softly.

Her mother looked down into her child's lap. "Fingers crossed? An old Browne habit?"

"He says—" She paused to lick her suddenly dry lips.

Her mother folded her hands and looked pleasantly at her. "He?"

"Ralph."

"Ralph says...?"

"Ralph says that if we want to get married it should be some simple ceremony—a judge, or a Justice of the Peace, or someone like that. In and out of his office, so to speak." Her eyes were glued to her shoes, and when her mother started to laugh her head snapped up indignantly.

"Mama? There's nothing funny about that, you know."

"Ah, but there is, my dear. When your father and I decided to marry...well, to be truthful about it, when your father decided we were to marry, that's just what I said. Something simple. Justice of the Peace, something like that."

"But—but you were married in the church."

"Of course we were. Four maids of honor, one matron of honor, one flower girl and Lord, you wouldn't believe how many dignitaries. I thought for the longest time that I was marrying Latimore Incorporated. And of course that was in the middle of winter, so there were Latimore snowplows and Latimore limousines, and a pair of four-wheel-drive cars just in case the snow got too deep, and one Latimore helicopter standing by just in case there was some sort of mix-up, and a bevy of Latimore security men just to help out the local police! You wouldn't believe!"

"Did you—enjoy it all, Ma?"

"Daughter, I had a marvelous time. I didn't realize it earlier but a wedding is for the bride, you know. She and her mother make the arrangements, her father pays all the bills, and then when the bride and groom go off all the rest sit down and put their feet up and—so they told me later—they all have a good couple of drinks and a good cry—"

"But you didn't have a mother! Or a father either!"

"Love, that's what I thought, but your father explained it all to me in small, simple words. Since I didn't have a mother, Latimore Incorporated stood in as my mother, and didn't she do me well?"

"Ma, I don't understand all this stuff about marrying. You said that the bride's mother pays all the bills? Or her father? And what does the groom do?"

"As best I remember, the groom needs a new suit and is required to attend on time. That's not too difficult, is it? But of course, after the wedding, he's responsible for the honeymoon and the happy-ever-after bit."

"I'll break his *other* leg! Damn man!"

"Are we perhaps moving out of the theoretical? Does the name Browne enter the picture?"

"Ma, I can't seem to help it. I love the—"

"Now, now. No cursing. Not at least until after the wedding. He did make you another offer?"

"Yes. And he was about as graceful as a bear. He said 'I've got a day off next Tuesday, so why don't we—?' I'll kill that man!" She quickly raised a hand to stab at a leaking eye, and reminded herself that she was *never* going to cry over that man again. Never. "Ma, did my father ever behave like that?"

"Like that, child? Why, you have it lucky, let me tell you. Your father, the Christmas before we were married, lost his temper completely, sent your sister Mattie off to Newport to live with her grandmother, and then rushed off to the Sahara desert to build another darn road. Just before Christmas—would you believe that? And he didn't come back until I told him that Mattie had run away in the middle of the biggest snowstorm in New England history and that... Oh, well, that's history, isn't it?"

"Did you—perhaps—say something to upset him?"

"Me?" Mary Kate, even after all those years, managed to work up a blush. "Well, I did mention a word or two about the Colonel, and then—" she stopped a moment to catch her breath "—and then told him I loved him."

"Just that? You loved him?"

"Just that. There really wasn't anything else to say. So what do you plan to do now, love?"

"Do? I'm going to leave Rex here. He's feeling his age. And I'm going back to that house and I'm going to raise all kinds of— Oh, Mrs Bethel, have you finished?"

"Yes, I believe so. And if you need more advice don't hesitate to contact Reverend Duncan. A fine young man. Very young, of course, but a fine young man."

"Yes, if I need more advice I'll be sure to call on Reverend Duncan."

The two Latimore women watched as Mrs Bethel wandered down the path and out the gate.

"And so you were saying...?" Mary Kate prompted.

"I was saying," Hope said firmly, "that I'll go back down the highway and I'll cloud up and rain all over that man!"

Hope got up, returned the trowel to her mother, and stomped down to the cemetery exit. Moments later Mary Kate heard the ragged roar of the engine of her youngest daughter's ancient Jeep. Then she heard two more cars come into the family parking lot beside the house.

"My goodness," Mary Kate Latimore murmured as she squirmed down into the uncomfortable iron seat and stared across to the back of the lovely old church. "How strong-willed *we* have become!" And she grinned, a very wry but self-satisfied grin.

Hope had prepared herself to roar off like an avenging angel, but before she could back out two cars came up, one on either side of her, pinning her into her parking space. Her father got out of one; her brother Michael climbed out of the other. Both wore accusing looks on their faces.

Michael was tall, heavy, impressive, and for years
Hope Latimore had walked in his shadow. He waved a
long sheet of paper in front of her as she climbed out
of her vehicle.

"Well?"

"Easy," her father murmured.

"Easy what?" Hope demanded.

"This is a bill to Latimore Incorporated for six
hundred thousand dollars," Michael said. "It says 'For
certain rescue operations in Sanjestan.' Now, I'd like to
know who authorized this. At the bottom it says, 'Authorized by Latimore family member.' Now, it wasn't
me or Dad, or Mattie, or Faith, and Becky never deals
in company business."

Hope stepped back a pace or two and shaded her eyes
from the sun. At well over six feet her only brother went
up a long, long way. "Six hundred thousand? We got
off cheap. I figured it might be a million five or so."

"Damn it, that's a lot of—" And he fell silent as his
father put a hand on his arm.

"For what, sweetheart?"

"Well, I had to rescue my prospective sister-in-law,"
she said firmly. "She and her husband were being held
hostage by a guerrilla group."

Her brother looked as though he might be swallowing
his tongue. Her father moved over to her and kissed her
forehead. "Well, now, as you say, it could easily have
gone a million five. Does your mother know about this?"

"About the rescue? No. About the prospective sister-
in-law, yes. I just told her. I—think I just told her. She's
over in the cemetery, laughing at me. Excuse me; I've
got to go straighten my man out."

And now her father was laughing at her too. And
her brother.

"At this price," Michael said, "it'll be worth it for me to come along with you and help out."

"No, thank you," Hope said in her most gentle voice. "I intend to take care of this all by myself. By the way, what does passel mean? Mama said she had a passel of things to do today."

"Old New England," her father said. "A passel means a whole bunch of things. But then she's always doing a passel of things, isn't she? And now it looks as if her baby daughter is growing up the same way."

Hope slid back into the driver's seat of her Jeep, and then leaned out the window. "Pa, I've told you and told you, I am *not* your *baby* daughter!"

Both of the men stepped out of the way as the Jeep jerked a couple of times and backed out onto the highway.

"Look who grew up today," her father said to his son. "Here comes your mother, wearing that Wicked Witch look of hers. I wonder—let's see if we can wangle a bite or two to eat."

Ralph Browne was still pacing the floor, up and down, from the kitchen to the front door and back again. Up and down, up and down, and all the time muttering.

"Where the devil could she have gone? No, that isn't right. Not where, but why? You tell a girl that we're going to get married and she snatches up her suitcase and stomps out of the house. Do you suppose there's a rejection in that? Or a firm maybe? If only the kids were here she'd be around like a shot!"

And then he heard a car come up into the drive. Not her cranky Jeep, not his sister's rental car. Who? He brushed a curtain aside on the porch and watched as tall, thin Alfred Pleasanton squeezed out of his gleaming Porsche. And not a second or two behind him came the worn black Jeep, clattering and moaning up the driveway alongside the house.

Ralph Browne ducked back into the living room, picked up the newspaper, and did his best to look busy. It wasn't all that hard. His housekeeper had been gone for barely an hour and the house already looked like a pigsty. The front doorlatch rattled.

"And if you don't take your hands off me, Alfred, I'm going to rearrange all those lovely teeth."

"You and who else?" Alfred retorted. "Dammit, stop trying to scratch my face."

"Alfred, turn me loose before I call my dog."

"Hah. I saw you leave the mutt at your mother's house. And those kids are back on Myrtle Street."

"Ralph is upstairs," she warned him, but he could hear the quaver in her voice.

"I doubt that."

Ralph wasn't, of course. He came up out of his chair, stretched, and came out into the hall. "What a clever fellow you are, Pleasanton. I wasn't upstairs at all. Why don't you turn the lady loose like she asked?"

"Look, Browne, the last time we met it was all an accident. If the kid hadn't brought in that gun you would never have had a chance. Why don't you just go back to your—" he looked over Ralph's shoulder and saw the scattered newspaper "—journal? I'm gonna tame this little witch, and then I'm gonna marry her. Or maybe I won't marry her. How's your leg, shorty? Dangerous things, broken legs."

"They really are," Ralph returned. "You know, that's a funny thing. I was almost positive *I* was going to marry the girl. In fact I was about to go over to ask her father about it."

Pleasanton flexed his fingers and dropped Hope's wrist. "A waste of time, Browne. I'm in good with the old man. And her mother as well."

"Hope, why don't you go into the kitchen and make me a cup of coffee?" Ralph suggested.

"You're sure y-you'll—be all right?" she stammered.

"I'll be all right," Ralph said, "but I can't say the same for Pleasanton here. You told your mother about us?" Hope nodded. "So what did she say?"

"She just—laughed."

"Smart woman," Alfred said. "Why don't you go make that coffee? Browne is going to need it."

"I—believe I will." Hope scurried down the corridor and turned around at the door just in time to see Ralph spring high in the air and kick out at Alfred's solar plexus. The tall, thin man bounced back against the wall and collapsed downward into a sitting position, and didn't make another move or say another word. Hope snatched at a skillet, which was grease-stained and dirty, and ran back up the corridor.

"I said—you shouldn't have done that. You'll ruin his nice new teeth. His mother will be *very* angry with you."

"Who, me? I never came close to those shiny new teeth of his. Besides, I was very disturbed by what he was saying to you. Drop the skillet."

She opened her tiny white hand and let the iron skillet fall to the floor. It bounced off the side of Pleasanton's head with a hollow thump and fell on the rug.

"And now come over here."

"Very bossy, aren't you?"

"Very."

She shook her head gently, but went to him all the same. It was hard to catch up to him because every time she took a step in his direction he seemed to move, stiff-

legged, backward, until finally his thighs touched his big
morris chair and he sat down.

"You remember all those things I said I was going to
do to you on our wedding night?" he queried. His mouth
clamped shut for a moment, and then a tiny smile
returned.

"Yes. Very threatening, they were. And?"

"Well, I'm not going to do any of them."

"Not any of them?" she asked suspiciously.

"Not any of them," he said, caressing his leg.

"Some of them sounded like a lot of fun."

"Some of them would have been. But no more."

"Why not, Ralph?"

"Why not? Because I just broke my other leg!"

Pleasanton groaned and struggled to sit up.

"I don't know about that," Hope said. "I'm not all
that sure that I want to marry a man with a broken leg."
She watched as Pleasanton tried to get to his feet.

"He could give us a little trouble." Ralph gestured to
the other man. "I don't think I could do that again—
that kick-boxing stuff."

"Not to worry," Hope Latimore said. And the smallest
of all the Latimore tribe straightened her skirt and walked
over to Alfred's side. "Come on, big guy." She offered
an arm to help him stagger up, and then gently guided
him to the front door and walked him out onto the porch.
"Have a good life," she told him, then removed her arm.
He wavered back and forth for a moment. She touched
him gently with the forefinger of her right hand.

Perhaps it was the weight of her finger, or perhaps it
was the little gust of wind that whistled around the north
side of the house. In any event Pleasanton slid off the
top step of the porch and flopped down into the patch
of mud just at the bottom of the steps. Hope admired
her work for a moment before going back to Ralph.

"What did you do?" he asked a little tentatively.

"Nothing much. I just pointed him toward his mother's house. He would have been fine, but he slipped in that mud patch by the stairs. You should have cleaned that up, you know. He might sue."

She waltzed by him, gathered her skirts under her, and relaxed on the couch. "Now, about *my* wedding . . ." she said primly.

CHAPTER ELEVEN

"*YOUR* wedding? I thought both of us were sharing this simple little ceremony? What is this, some sort of palace revolution? I thought I had this all straightened out. We're going to get married, and I'm going to be wearing the pants in this family."

"Ralph Browne," she snapped at him, "I've never, ever said a thing about who's wearing what. You will certainly be the head of our family. And I guarantee I will respect every—most of—your commandments." She shifted her position slightly to allow for crossed fingers on both her hands. "And the only thing I require is that I will name all the girl children. There's nothing wrong with that, is there?"

"I find it hard to tell," he muttered. "My foot hurts. Do you suppose you could call one of your medical relatives, or the emergency service, or—?"

"Of course I will," she said sweetly. And she did. "They'll be a little while," she informed him a moment later. "Just don't wiggle so much." And then, in a gentle, conversational tone, she said, "Did you know that the bride's mother and father are responsible for paying for the wedding?"

"Not to worry," he grumbled. "It'll be cheap. Just a Justice in his office. I don't mind paying."

"Ah. That's good of you, but we'll have to be careful about the scheduling."

"Why's that?"

"Because I'm going to be married in a church, with a full ceremony, flowers and music and all that. Just so

174

long as you don't plan this ceremony in the Justice's office so that it conflicts with mine, everything will be just fine.''

"I have a feeling," he said slowly, "that there's something going on behind the woodwork. It must be because my leg hurts. *You're* going to have a church wedding? Flowers and long white gloves, and bridesmaids, and all that stuff?''

"And a flower girl. I haven't asked Melody yet, but I'm sure she'll accept."

"Now just a damn minute! I told you we were going to be married by a Justice."

"I heard you the first time you said it, Ralph."

"And we're not going to have some screwy double ceremony. Not!"

"I don't see why not. In France they have a civil ceremony and then a religious ceremony. And I don't see why we can't do the same."

"I said—!"

"Careful, Ralph. You've got to hold onto your temper or you'll do yourself some damage." She cocked her head toward the front door. "Ambulance," she commented.

"No double ceremonies," he growled. The ambulance was coming down the State highway full throttle and with siren screaming.

"I love it when you growl," she said, giggling.

"No double ceremonies," he repeated.

Hope sighed and folded both hands in her lap. "Too bad," she said. "Then I'll just have to find myself another man, won't I? Maybe I could go back to Eastport and see what I can find." She shook her head dolefully. "Well, I suppose you'll have to get your sister to come and take care of you too." She blinked a couple of times at him, but was unable to work up a tear. "I'm sorry now that I sent Alfred off. He's not as nice as you, but a girl can't be too particular."

She whipped a handkerchief out of his pocket and dabbed at her perfectly dry eyes. And then she stood up and went to the door to let the paramedics into the house.

"Browne again?" The chief shook his head sadly.

"Yes."

"They gave him the lecture, you know. Break the same leg twice and there's liable to be all sorts of trouble for him."

"He heard it, but he just couldn't see his way clear. This time he reckons he's broken the *other* leg. It's that Japanese fighting stuff. A sort of challenge to his manhood, I guess. You're both about his size. Is that the sort of reaction one should expect from a shorter man?"

"Woman!" Ralph Browne snarled again. Fiercely enough to put the fear of God into Hope Latimore's soul.

"Yes, sir?"

"I'm going to the hospital."

"Yes, sir."

"When I come back there's going to be a considerable amount of silence around these parts. And when I say, Jump, the only thing I expect you to say is, 'How high, sir?' "

"Yes—yes, sir."

"And then I'm going to consult with your mother, and you and I are going to get married. You hear?"

"I—yes, sir. She'll like that. My mother, I mean. She loves consultations. And weddings too."

"Shut up!"

"Yes, sir. Do I get to kiss you before they carry you away?"

"I suppose, but don't be too snippity about it."

*　　*　　*

In just one week the old church had been modified to fit the need. A temporary wooden ramp had been built over the steps and given a quick coat of white paint. The same sort of ramp was constructed over the stairs of the Latimore house.

In one more week a tiny woman had been fitted into a delightful wedding dress—a sparkling confection of white silk with a taffeta petticoat to provide a little rustle. It almost reached the floor, but was long enough to disguise her four-inch heels. Then—to please the groom—there was a deep-dipping bodice to illustrate that she was indeed no child. A thin gold coronet sat jauntily atop her upswept hair and supported the veil of mist that barely reached to her shoulders.

"And you'll really love it all," Hope assured Ralph, after describing the dress in detail the day before the wedding.

"No demonstration?" he asked.

"No demonstration," Hope said firmly. "I've told you and told you, I don't give samples."

"Spoilsport."

The four of them were sitting in the living room of the old Latimore mansion in Eastport, the older couple sharing the capacious love-seat and Hope in her mother's rocking chair, huddled up close to Ralph's wheelchair. At this juncture Mary Kate stood up and tugged at her husband's sleeve. "Time we went upstairs," she coaxed.

Bruce grinned at her. "But we're just getting to the interesting part," he complained.

"I'll show you *interesting*." His wife jerked on his sleeve again. "We're getting old, Mr Latimore, and we both need a little nap. Upstairs in my *interesting* room." And off they went.

"I wonder what she meant by that?" Ralph Browne mused.

"So you'll find out next week, when you're older," Hope teased.

"That's a promise?"

"Solemn oath." Hope crossed her heart, hiding her other hand—the one with the crossed fingers—behind her.

"I have a funny feeling about all this," he said. "I wouldn't want you to think that you're going to rule our home the way your mother rules this one."

"I wouldn't dream of it," Hope said meekly. "And my mother never did rule the house when we were all young. Don't make the mistake of thinking my pop is a pushover. He's in charge of everything and everybody! Full time."

"Yeah, I can believe that, girl. Well, almost believe that. Come here."

Hope got up hesitantly. "Why?"

"Don't ask foolish questions. Just come here."

She stood a pace or two away from him and bent over his wheelchair. "And?"

He seized her with two strong hands and pulled her over into his lap.

"Hey. Be careful."

"I have a broken leg," he lectured solemnly. "There's absolutely nothing wrong with the rest of me." And he began to demonstrate, pulling her close against him and kissing her with a gentle passion that gradually increased. When he finally turned her loose she was breathless, her cheeks blush-red, her mind just the tiniest bit scatter-shot.

"Well, really," she protested.

"Yes, really. Don't struggle; I might drop you."

"You wouldn't dare?" It had started out as a strong statement and ended up as a querulous question.

"Oh, I'd dare," he said, chuckling. "I might not accomplish it all, but I'd dare, believe me." His hand moved up to the zipper at the top of her dress.

"What—?"

The tiny gold zipper slipped downward.

"Don't *do* that," she snapped, trying to stop the movement of the metal with no success.

"I'll do anything I please," he retorted as the zipper opened, revealing her full breasts. "And this pleases you very much." He nuzzled her. "My, that is nice." He nuzzled at her some more, then kissed her thoroughly.

"Don't do that," she snarled at him. "What if my parents—?" And then the doorbell rang.

Hope tried to squirm out of his lap, but he held her fast. "I told you not to—" she gasped. The bell rang again.

"Ralph Browne!"

"Oh, hush," he teased. "Whoever it is will think there's nobody home and will go away. Probably an encyclopedia salesman."

But it wasn't and they didn't. The door popped open, and a tiny cheerful voice said, "Uncle Ralph, where is you?" And Melody Jakowski scooted around the corner into the room, followed in a more leisurely fashion by her mother.

"Mommy and me is come to visit, Aunty Hope. What is you doin'?"

"Your aunty has something stuck in her eye," Ralph said. "It's probably an eyelash or something and I'm trying to get it out. Hi, Eloise."

"Hi, brother. Eyelash? Hah!"

"Is that all you have to say? Hah? Look, I took care of your two—children—for months, and now, in my hour of need—"

"Hour of need, hah!"

"Shut up, sister. Where was I?"

"Hour of need," Hope prompted.

"Yes, in my hour of need all I get is a hah! You don't believe I was trying to help Hope get an eyelash cleared away out of my love for her?"

"Hope?"

"If I were still a Latimore I suspect even I would be a little—just a little—doubtful. But tomorrow afternoon I'm going to become a Browne. So—" She stopped for a deep breath. "So I'm forced to tell you that everything Ralph has to say about our relationship is absolutely honest, sincere and relevant."

"Good Lord, has he ever got you trained! A whip and gun, like the lion tamers?"

"Not me," Hope protested. "I've never been a lion. Or lioness. Whatever. All I know is what my mother told me."

"Smart lady, your mother," Eloise said. "What did she tell you?"

Hope struggled out of Ralph's lap, and then, almost as if reciting a catechism, stated, "Every family has to have a head. Ralph is going to be the head of our family. I'm going to do everything he tells me. Except if he tells me to do something that I absolutely disagree with. And then I'm going to put my heels down and dig in the dirt with all my strength, and do just what I want to."

"What a crazy, mixed-up pair you two are," Eloise said, sighing. "Well, that's life, I guess. Now, it's five after eleven."

"Is that so?" Ralph checked his wristwatch. "Ever since that little argument I had with Alfred Pleasanton I haven't been able to get my watch running right. Almost an hour till lunchtime?"

"Almost five past the hour when we were all going to meet at the church for a quick rehearsal of this wedding you keep talking about."

"I knew there was something you forgot about," Hope chided him.

"*I* forgot about? Where do you get this *I* forgot about? You'll remember I said we ought to just find ourselves a Justice of the Peace—but no, we have to have a church wedding with all that phony baloney."

"An' now we is late for the—the—" Melody paused, uncertain.

"Rehearsal," her aunt Hope said.

"That big man over at the church is gettin' mad and—"

"My brother—Michael."

"Yes, your big brother Michael."

Hope nodded. It was hard keeping a straight face.

"Yes, him. An' he said you better haul your—"

"That's enough, Melody," her mother said sharply. "Ladies don't say things like that. Big brothers might, but ladies don't."

The little girl pondered for a moment, and then said wearily, "Aunty Hope, s'awful hard bein' a lady, ain't it?"

"You'd better believe it," her currently adoptive aunt said glumly.

"So all right," Michael said. "I'll have the ramp fixed."

"When?" Hope glared up at her brother and stamped her foot in the deep bronze carpet, with absolutely no effect at all. "I almost rolled Ralph off the edge."

"If you'll remember, baby sister, I offered to push the wheelchair and you blew your stack."

Hope took a deep breath. "I did *not*," she said fiercely, "blow my stack. Ralph doesn't like me to do that sort of thing. And let me remind you I am not *your* baby sister. You are *my* baby brother!''

"Hope," her brother-in-law, Jake Meadows, cautioned, "be nice to your baby brother. He's a very sensitive young man."

"S-sensitive? Like a p-piece of granite," Hope stuttered.

"Hope," Ralph Browne said mildly from the depths of his wheelchair. A silence fell over the little group standing at the church entrance.

Hope Latimore, her mouth half-open, managed to close it and take another deep breath.

"But...' she protested.

"Hush up," her prospective husband commented gently. "I never did like gabby women."

The small group all grinned. All except Hope. Michael took control of the wheelchair and started it down the ramp.

"See you tomorrow afternoon," Reverend Duncan said heartily. "Two o'clock."

Hope Latimore, lingering behind the group, muttered to her sister Faith, who had flown in from the Caribbean especially for the wedding, "I don't have to put up with that, do I?"

"I don't know, love. If you want the gain you have to put up with the pain."

"I could always go into the convent," Hope said firmly.

"I'll surely believe that," her sister muttered. "On the next February thirty-first." She stopped halfway down the ramp and tugged at her tiny sister's sleeve.

"Well, I will!"

"Of course you will, dear." And a pause ensued as Faith tried to think of a polite way of asking something. "Hope, are you, perhaps, still a virgin?"

"Why, of course I am. I'm supposed to be. That's the name of the game," Hope responded indignantly.

Her sister shook her head. "Twenty-four years old and still—"

"What—what's that got to do with anything?" Hope interrupted.

"Oh, nothing, really," Faith returned. "I thought perhaps you might be a little nervous about the physical aspect of marriage. But of course you aren't?"

Hope nodded affirmatively. Me, afraid? she told herself. What a silly idea. Mama told me everything. Absolutely everything?

"But early in the morning, the day after tomorrow, I want you to call me up and we'll talk about the convent," Faith said. "All right?"

Hope shrugged and followed behind the procession as everyone else climbed into their cars. She found Ralph and his wheelchair parked next to her brother's big Mercedes, all alone. "What kept you?" he asked. There was a gentleness in the asking, a sort of verbal caress that rushed up from the base of her spine and ran higher, into the center of her mind. "You've been delegated to be my driver."

"How did that ever happen? I thought my sister Mattie had been assigned to do the dirty work?"

He grinned up at her. "Don't ask me. I can't fathom the mind of the baby of the family, so how do you expect me to understand the older? I saw Mattie and Faith whispering to each other, and then Faith came over and said you were to be my chauffeur."

It was almost an automatic reaction. "I am *not* the baby of the family," she said as she opened the passenger-side door. "And how do I get you inside this thing?"

"I've one good leg," he said. "Loan me your shoulder." He set the brake on the chair and pulled himself up on one leg. Obediently she stepped close, and was immediately pinned against his side by the power of one arm. It was amazing. At five feet eight he would have rated in most people's minds as a small man, but his muscle power was relatively as great as that of all the big men in the family.

"You'll have to help me move," he murmured in her nearest ear. "I don't do any flying these days." And so she helped him over to the open car door, where he slipped into the seat with all the grace of a ballet dancer, leaving Hope with empty arms and an astonished gasp emerging from her throat.

She had more trouble with the wheelchair, but, having refused all the offered help, she finally managed to get it folded up and stuffed in the boot of the car. When she slid into the driver's seat she had another moment of embarrassment. The seat was adjusted for Michael's long legs.

"There's an adjustment lever under the left side," Ralph coached. "Turn the motor on. Everything in cars like this is power-driven."

"You know everything, don't you?" she whispered.

"Not quite," he returned as the car engine began its muted sound. "Slide over here." She complied, all her normal rebellious notions suppressed.

"Kiss me," he ordered.

"But—but the whole family is watching."

"And half the neighborhood and the church choir," he said, chuckling. "But I have a license for it." He tapped his coat pocket.

So how could I refuse? Hope asked herself. But nevertheless she wished for curtains, or drapes, or a quiet bedroom. And then a warm arm came around her, and turned her sidewise in the seat.

"Like this," he murmured, and before she could think of a word or phrase his lips were sealed on hers, searching, and Hope Latimore forgot all the things the good sisters at the Catholic high school had ever taught her about what good girls did *not* do in either the front *or* back seats of cars. And then, after taking five minutes to recuperate, she prepared to drive the big car down the State highway.

As they pulled out of the church parking lot she could hear the burring of saws and the thunder of hammers as her brother Michael kept his word about rebuilding the ramp. Hope smiled at the thought. After all, albeit for hours now rather than days, she was *still* a Latimore. For a short time, perhaps, but still a Latimore. The trembling disappeared from her arms as she awkwardly pursed her lips and whistled a little tune which she only half remembered.

"Don't do that," Ralph corrected. "It's bad luck—whistling girls and barking dogs—things like that."

"Hah!" she snorted as she turned the car up into the driveway at the Browne house.

"Hah, hell!" Ralph said. "I told you—bad luck. Whose car is that?"

"Your sister's," she told him glumly.

"Yes, and both her kids are standing on the porch," he muttered. "I had hoped that—"

"Me too," Hope broke in as she slammed on the brakes.

Eloise came out of the house and ran down the stairs. She and Melody had left the church rehearsal as soon as Melody's part in it was over. "Thank the Lord you two showed up." Hope lowered her window.

"Trouble?"

"I have to take Harry back to the hospital. It's his foot—and there's nowhere to put the kids, so I thought—You're not too busy until tomorrow afternoon, and you certainly wouldn't mind. They're still pretty excitable, but—" And by that time Eloise, come yea or nay, was halfway down the drive to her car.

Melody replaced her mother at the car window. "Well, is you 'sprised?" She grinned.

"Yes, I guess I'm surprised," Hope said. "But, well, that's what uncles are for, right?"

Melody nodded. Eddie came down the steps. "But I got a ball game this afternoon," he complained. "And I ain't got no ride to the field."

"No problem," Hope said as she opened the car door. "Let me get your uncle into the house, and Melody can be his nurse while I take you to the game. Won't that be fun?"

"Yeah," Ralph Browne grumbled. "That will certainly be fun."

"You is a good nuncle," Melody told him.

And so they all prodded and poked and nagged until nice Uncle Ralph was comfortably settled on the couch in the living room, then Eddie and all his equipment were piled into the Mercedes.

"I don't even get lunch?" Ralph asked when Hope ran in to tell him they were ready to go.

"The game starts in thirty minutes," she told him.

"I is gonna make you lunch," Melody promised. "Cold oatmeal, on account of I'm not 'sposed to turn on the stove."

"Gee, thanks," her nice uncle said grimly. "Hurry back, Hope," he pleaded. And though he could not see an ounce of humor in it all Hope laughed as she ran back down the steps to the car.

* * *

She was still fighting back a nervous grin as she stood at the head of the aisle the next afternoon, her hand on her father's arm, and Ralph in his wheelchair, some thousand miles away down the aisle, looking desperate. As was she. Nothing had worked last night. The ball game had run overtime, Eloise hadn't returned until eleven-thirty, Ralph had fallen asleep by ten o'clock, and she'd been unable to wake him up after all the people had left.

As a result, she told herself, I'm still the virgin bride, and I don't dare tell my father because he'll laugh! And the music started.

Melody was the flower girl. Instead of preceding the maids of honor, as soon as the music started she skipped up in front of the bride and started snatching petals from her bouquet of baby roses. Every five or six steps along she would stop and hand a couple of petals to whomever was sitting in the pews. Halfway down the aisle she found a genial friend, to whom she gave half the roses still remaining. "That's my mama," she said, loud enough to be heard in Boston, some fifty miles away.

Reverend Duncan was young, lovable, had no children, and had two more weddings to follow. Melody, standing determinedly between the bride and the groom at the altar, felt he needed help with the liturgy. So it was a laughingly late congregation that gathered at the church door and wished the bridal couple well as Michael wheeled the chair down the ramp, being sure to call his little sister's attention to the improvements provided overnight.

The reception was held in the town hall on Main Street. Everyone in town came. And some of their out-of-town relatives. After the first hour of revelry Mary Kate came over to her youngest daughter. "Your husband looks pretty worn out," she said. Said at a yell, of course. The band had only one praiseworthy attribute. It played louder than the guests could sing.

And so some four participants helped them down the stairs to their car. Three of them carried Ralph—and his wheelchair—over to their car. Michael picked up Hope at the foot of the ramp, swung her around in a couple of dizzy whirls and stuffed her into the family Mercedes. A small group of other guests stood close by, watching the proceedings.

"Where are you going on your honeymoon?" Eloise called. She had just sprinkled rice all over Hope's beautiful dress. Most of it had gone down the valley of Hope's bosom. It felt like taking a bath in sand.

"I'm not telling," Hope returned.

And at the same moment her brand-new husband muttered, "Home to bed."

And so they went home and did. Go to bed, that was.

With all the doors locked, and Rex standing guard on the porch, and only one lamp lit in the living room—which had once again been converted into a hospital room—Hope Latimore Browne confronted her biggest problem.

"Ralph?"

"Yes, dear."

"I—still don't know how to do it."

"I do, love."

The instructions took three minutes; the execution of them lasted most of the night. They both fell asleep at approximately two in the morning, worn out.

And the first thing Hope Browne did when she awoke was reach for the telephone.

"What the devil are you up to now?" Ralph asked.

"I have to talk to Faith."

"Your sister?"

"My sister."

"Why?"

"That, Mr. Browne, is none of your business, but I did promise I would call her this morning and talk about entering a convent."

"Entering a—what? Why on earth do you want to talk to her about that?"

Hope Browne stretched like a luxuriating little cat who knew full well how to do it. "I want to tell her," she said, "that I'm not going. Want to try that again?"